Bridge Mix

Chocolate-covered contracts
and plenty of nuts

Paul Holtham
Foreword by David Silver

Master Point Press • Toronto, Canada

Text © 2011 Paul Holtham
Cover image © Olena Sullivan

All rights reserved. It is illegal to reproduce any portion of this material, except by special arrangement with the publisher. Reproduction of this material without authorization, by any duplication process whatsoever, is a violation of copyright.

Master Point Press
331 Douglas Ave.
Toronto, Ontario, Canada
M5M 1H2   (416)781-0351
Email: info@masterpointpress.com
Websites: www.masterpointpress.com
             www.masteringbridge.com
             www.bridgeblogging.com
             www.ebooksbridge.com

Library and Archives Canada Cataloguing in Publication

Holtham, Paul
Bridge mix : chocolate-covered contracts and plenty of nuts / Paul Holtham.
Short stories.
Issued also in electronic formats.

ISBN 978-1-897106-74-7

       1. Contract bridge--Fiction. 2. Canadian wit and humor (English).
I. Title.
PS8615.O4814B75 2011   C813'.6   C2010-906865-3

We acknowledge the financial support of the Government of Canada through the Book Publishing Industry Development Program (BPIDP) for our publishing activities.

Editor   Ray Lee
Interior format   Sally Sparrow
Cover and interior design   Olena S. Sullivan/New Mediatrix

1 2 3 4 5 6 7   14 13 12 11 10
PRINTED IN CANADA

Foreword

And now, something completely different. A bridge book that combines frenetic pacing with exotic characters and interesting deals. *Bridge Mix* is a psychedelic trip through various bridge competitions as it might be told by Ford Prefect living his hallucinations in real time. But Paul Holtham's book makes *A Hitchhiker's Guide to the Galaxy* seem like *Alice in Wonderland*. Holtham achieves his stunning effects through two devices—style and characterization—each complementing the other to produce an engrossing, delightful narrative.

Holtham's style is evocative, but not imitative. Here is an incident from the beginning of the book.

> With maximum weirdness, the paper descended back into reading range. It crumpled into my knees like the Hindenberg going down, minus the combustion. Then my fists came to rest and the top accordioned open. I gazed upon the Cheeseburger Diet to Health. Reluctantly (very reluctantly; it was the single bravest act of my life) I stretched the pages apart and willed my gaze to follow the flattening wrinkles outward across the left one.

The euphony and rhythm of the sentences are pleasing to the reader because of the author's skill in handling the words, both familiar and unusual, in vivid imagery, e.g. "accordioned open", "Cheeseburger Diet". The well-read bridge player will vaguely recall seeing this style before — William Faulkner's "The Bear" is a classic example, but frankly, I prefer Holtham to Faulkner. Holtham has a mischievous talent for inventing words that fit neatly into his narrative and enhance the reader's enjoyment. He also is skilled in adapting his style to the context of his story. The hands being played are described in a stream-of-consciousness real time. Eavesdropping on an expert's thought processes as he plays a hand, trying to get a count by evaluating the spot cards played and adjusting his game plan to the developments revealed, or implied, by the play of the cards is a refreshing and informative mode of presentation. I found it far more enjoyable than the usual arcane discussion of probabilities, odds, and technicalities in most bridge books, including my own.

The characters in *Bridge Mix* are stranger than the customers in Chalmun's Cantina, *Star Wars'* watering hole for galactic aliens. Egyptian gods, Norse gods, aliens with strange shapes and bidding systems, all sit down at the table during the weirdest Individual event ever held in a bridge tournament. They all have individuality and all are skillful and aggressive opponents. And just when our hero, and the reader, begins to understand them we are teleported to another game in an even more outlandish location to face another quartet of foes from the Galactic Bridge Federation.

The action never stops, and the reader never tires of it.

David Silver
January 2011

Halloween	7
The Pyramid Scheme	37
Close Encounters of the Unkind	63
Aliens	91
Weird Scenes Inside the Ol' Mind	115

#

It was a dark and stormy night. Really. A chilly, totally dreary All Hallows Eve. And my birthday to boot. *New England sure is a chip off the old block*, I thought sourly, and winced as the Sheraton's vast, depopulated lobby blanched to radioactive whiteness. An instant later it convulsed with the latest and most murderous blast in Thor's drive-by shooting spree. He was not exclusively the L.A. god of thunder.

Worse, the accompanying deluge was solid; it would have made Noah curse God for not telling him to build a submarine, and it acted like a hydraulic press. The megawatt discharges down into the lobby's climate-controlled air formed a corrosive concoction that singed my nose hairs and stung my eyes.

I was skimming through a cheesy tabloid someone had actually bought. Another day, another Elvis sighting. I burped unhappily. After an indigestible hotel supper, and unable to go for a therapeutic walk, I was killing time before the evening session of the Individual. Aside from everything else, I had a malignant bridge hangover that kept me trying to sort the lightning flashes into suits. Oh yes, and the couch was trying to eat me.

I cursed the cheapskate gene that left me unable to fork over money for a room just for the day. A soft, roomy bed to hide under was paradise lost. Being away from people for free was the one advantage the current ambience provided, though the result wasn't exactly solitude.

I found myself eyeing the alcove beside my couch, wherein a quarter-guzzling, randomly dispensing Coke machine, a caffeine junkie's last resort, hawked its wares. Its location was friendly to would-be vandals; the alcove didn't face the front desk, which was practically over the horizon anyway. A miniature rain forest loomed behind me — vicariously glorying in the deluge, damn its imitation primeval heart — and was ringed with nice fist-sized rocks.

Esthetics were the main reason I hadn't resorted to vandalism yet: the glowing white ENJOY ICE-COLD SPRITE command, one of several parading across the machine's pop-bellied abdomen, was missing the R and E in SPRITE.

I shifted uncomfortably. The shriekingly yellow Naugahyde lounge, mounted on spindly chrome legs that *crouched*, may have looked like a humungous comfort insect, but it behaved like a carnivorous plant. Like others of its species, it secreted a perspiration-like substance that lulled its victim into thinking he was merely a bit too warm while the exudate ate through clothes and skin to get at his vitals. It would surely tear off great swatches of flesh if said victim panicked and bolted. Deadly, but since their diet consisted mainly of salesmen and conventioneers, not totally unappreciated.

For a while I had needed only to squirm sporadically, but the damned thing had worked itself into a feeding frenzy, and now I had to do it every thirty seconds or so to avoid becoming dinner. I was already a few ounces lighter thanks to some lapses. The ferns behind me rustled impatiently across the back of my neck, exasperated at my selfishness in shifting our paper around.

The fact that I remained hunkered down in a backwater of what had incrementally evolved into the world's worst theme park (Perfect Storm Land! Come for the heart-pounding terror! Stay for the corrosive asphyxiation!) should have told me something about the damage being done to my brain chemistry.

Outside, the rest of the downtown core had been sheared away by a capricious power failure. Between discharges, all that was visible from the couch was a shivery patch of sidewalk and two dead gooseneck streetlamps. Whenever Thor cut loose, a massive Victorian stone courthouse across the street fluoresced gaily in and out of existence. The city beyond became a murky twentieth-century Brigadoon on drugs.

A whole volley of explosions slammed through the glass, rippling it like cellophane. *Eek*. I wheezed, vibrated, and wheezed some more. *The Coke machine! Now!* But my muscles had gone deaf, and I perforce succumbed to fatalism. Ozone poisoning couldn't be the best way to go, but I figured I'd be well preserved, possibly in an interesting color. Then the most virulent fusillade to date irradiated the tabloid with a harsh phosphorescent vibrance. No mercy. It seemed to go on forever. But before I could get myself together and dump the blinding blarney back onto the glass coffee table and give everyone's eyes a break, a dark *something* squiggled over in the left page at the edge of my vision. Left. Sinister.

Like stenciling pulling loose from the bottom of a luminous white swimming pool, three wavering lines of ghostly black letters billowed up toward me.

Overtop both pages.

Out past the margins.

Into the quivering, ion-charged air.

Now the size of Second Coming headlines, they floated threateningly a foot away at eye level, a spectral billboard announcing a new reality. Words leered, registered. I knew what I was squinting at.

My horoscope. The one section I hadn't been desperate enough to read.

'Fortune will favor you, Virgo,' it prophesied. 'But be wary. An old family friend will try to deceive you.'

Ever been in a car accident, the kind where you bleed a lot? Then you know the sequence: an indeterminate interval of numbing, incapacitating shock; then denial, followed by (the interval depending on how much is poking out of you that shouldn't be) wild acceptance and an adrenaline rush that balloons your arteries while you fight to be calm, analytical, in control. My forehead once had a thirty-mile-per-hour introduction to my car's windshield, and the millrace of emotions was repeating now, only now I was mortally afraid my sanity had plowed right through the barrier between reality and the place where Cronenberg films are documentaries. Back then I'd stumbled past row after row of brightly lit houses on a bitter winter night to end up detailing my predicament into an out-of-order pay phone. I was coping less effectively this time. Paranoia was an ice-cold blade at my sphincter as brain-jarring reports smashed holes in space and time, non-stop. One ka-boom — two ka-booms

Seconds trudged by while its heavy, suffocating tympani continued kicking lobby butt... and trailed away.

The apparition was no less intimidating for want of a sound track, but it soon began losing cohesion and disintegrated into harmless black whorls. They faded to paler and paler gray... until I was left staring glassily at a perfectly ordinary newspaper being crinkled to death

Halloween | 9 |

at the end of rigidly outthrust arms. I was inclined to stay that way too; atavistic rigor has always served me well, dating from childhood nights when Grandma's Art Deco walnut dresser would mutate into a ten-eyed, soul-hungry emissary of Satan.

The couch was not interested in granting me a reprieve. I had to perform the requisite cheek roll, which led to my hyper-extended arms sagging at my elbows, then my shoulders. With maximum weirdness, the paper descended back into reading range. It crumpled into my knees like the Hindenburg going down, minus the combustion. Then my fists came to rest and the top accordioned open. I gazed upon the Cheeseburger Diet to Health.

Reluctantly (very reluctantly; it was the single bravest act of my life) I stretched the pages apart and willed my gaze to follow the flattening wrinkles outward across the left one.

Thank God. My brain hadn't gone completely freelance. There they were. The same words. Only now they were lying flat on the page in their little printy way, inert, innocuous... inane.

Good thing they don't say, 'You'll be roadkill in an hour', I thought distractedly. I squeezed out an Errol Flynn devil-may-care chuckle. Grace under pressure. Then why was I hearing Don Knotts whinny? Bad. Hysteria under pressure. Reflexively I swiveled my head — safe, it wasn't touching the couch — to see if anyone had come within eyeshot of my madness. Only the ferns, and true to form they were busy feigning indifference to the wild-eyed weirdo even as they subtly stiffened and pulled away.

I jerked my paranoia back to where it belonged and was grateful to see the horoscope hadn't roused from its lethargy. The fear that I would live out the rest of my life as a whacko dwindled appreciably once I knew the words themselves weren't imaginary, but how had I acquired their movie rights? In the frantic early seconds when I'd thought I could maybe blink the swirling nightmare away, optical illusion had been one hellaciously attractive theory. After being flayed by epileptic fluorescent lights all afternoon and then being cauterized by gigavolts of lightning, why *wouldn't* my frazzled optic nerves mutiny?

Alas, the image had lasted too long; my eyes had recorded it too faithfully. An *über*chill curdled my supper. Had the Stepin Fetchit feets-don't-fail-me-now S-S-Supernatural finally surfaced in my reality

— meaning my reality had always been a sham? Or, more rationally if not more believably, had the stupendous confluence of all that lightning forged a fistula that commingled our universe with one where the Supernatural *was* physics? And how long might *that* last?

Having Halloween go on forever because it was reality struck the fear gong harder than did the idea of being whacko — even major whacko, not reasonably benign and easily medicated whacko. Both prospects were terrifying, but a vision of me lugging a Saturday night special around town and sticking up 7-11s in order to support my new friends at the psychic hotline added the extra element of mortification.

Brrr.

Unfortunately the horoscope had a credential aside from its Hammer Message-From-Beyond presentation.

It described my still-to-come afternoon session.

Alcoholic honorary-uncle Rodney, he who'd introduced me to bridge — and other pastimes — had bumped into me in the morning (bumped, literally; he wasn't a morning person) and separated me from a twenty for whichever addiction proved more pressing.

He employed a typical cock-and-bull story about leaving his wallet in a taxi. He put the twenty in his wallet. He was a good soul, well worth the tithe — even for me — but it was a mystery how he'd gotten into my parents' circle, because they considered indulgences like alcohol or card-playing barely a cut above pedophilia. I got frostbite at family get-togethers and I was generally sober. Did his harmless and mutually understood prevarication count as deception? Iffy. But Fortune, well, Fortune had favored the hell out of me that morning, to the tune of three boards above average.

The opponents hadn't exhibited unusual largesse, for an Individual, but my partners hadn't sprayed the room with matchpoints either. There were none of the usual horror stories: no tinpot messiah bidding king-empty seventh to the skies, relentlessly ignoring the strain on your ethics as you try to keep from shrieking your doubles of the opponents' suit (your hundred honors); no deal where the opponents had more trumps than I did. My suits were led on defense and no free-range trumps were left to roam when my partners were on play. On top of all that, my own opening leads were survivable, the odd endplay actually made a difference, and I had guessed two queens.

Halloween | 11 |

Two queens? I gulped. I wished I hadn't remembered that. *Rats.* Everything seemed hell-bent on authenticating the tabloid drivel — including, I abruptly realized, the way I hadn't heard from Thor after he'd ushered in the weirdness. The sibilant baying of his rain hounds was missing, too.

I had some serious gibbering to do.

Somewhere along the line, the witches' brew my lungs had been sipping at had reverted to the standard undernourished air substitute Westinghouse kept a half-step ahead of Legionnaires' disease — and it was a honeyed milkshake going down my throat. My lungs became bellows. I could feel my brain becoming less and less of a fogbank as it got to metabolize oxygen instead of ozone.

Hmm. Ozone. Ozone narcosis. Rhymed with wishful diagnosis, but if I never looked it up it could never be ruled out, could it?

Aarrgghh. I'd had enough. Of the couch, the horoscope, the ferns, the lobby, the funk I was in. I needed time and distance. *Abandon ship.* Adrenaline spurted, inertia splintered, and I yanked myself to my feet, ignoring the pain of the skin toll to *Plasticus carnivorous*. I bequeathed the paper to the ferns (less than grateful, as you might expect), and stalked off toward the elevators. Rabbiting out of the front door would have been my preference, but I knew I couldn't, not unless I wanted to be haunted by the horoscope and its attendant goings-on forever. To manufacture the jumbo quantities of pooh needed to pooh-pooh them, I needed to go back to the killing fields, play my guts out, and have a forty percent game. Eat one for the Gipper. It wasn't like there was no precedent for it, and I was, for want of a better word, hopeful. Sitting through deal after deal being afraid that my suits wouldn't break badly or that my opponents would screw up would be strange though, sort of like walking into a final exam and hoping none of the questions you'd studied for were on it.

Still, what a waste of a great afternoon session. Either way, my bar tab was going to be unwieldy.

Three hours later, going into the last round, the afternoon session had repeated itself.

And to my surprise I wasn't a wreck. My psyche had rebounded like flubber. I guess *bingo!* phobia has a short half-life. Again there had been few outright gifts; mostly I'd had the steady returns that had matchpointed so well before. While back-to-back magic sessions in an Individual aren't the ego steroids they are in the Reisinger, they can flush a lot of self-doubt out of your system. That my results had been preordained by ability rather than fate was... believable. I suppose even winning the Irish sweepstakes eventually engenders a sense of entitlement. Besides, I'd had a revelation about my supernatural — note the small s — revelation: I'd dreamed it. Sound and fury notwithstanding, I'd fallen asleep — a micro-sleep — and my omnivorous subconscious had animated the part of the paper I hadn't consciously paid attention to. So simple, really. Why didn't I think of it before? It beat the hell out of ozone narcosis.

I could have my glorious triumph and eat it too.

Just keep riding the wave and don't blow your wee brainies out, I admonished the bleary-eyed goblin I'd been startled to see staring out at me from the washroom mirror. I'd known I was bit ragged around the edges, but I looked like a Gahan Wilson cartoon. Next I discovered I was glowing with a low-grade fever, and immediately more symptoms began jostling to get to the head of the line. The winner was my incipient facial stubble, a mass of parasitic eggs hatching. Plunging my head into a toilet and flushing — *cold, cold, swirling water* — actually crossed my mind. Instead slathering on facefuls of cold tap water seemed like a cop-out, but the tap water provided a palliative for my mood. I felt less like emergency-room fodder as I headed back out. To table thirteen.

From a distance, as I clumsily flamencoed through the checkerboard of white-skirted tables, my destination looked to be occupied by a pair of psychedelic dandelions. Before whimsy reverted to paranoia I was within a few tables and the Disney aura imploded. It left a reassuringly down-to-earth if depressing tableau of two vitrified geezesses (harsh, but a lifetime in the status trenches, masterpoint or otherwise, had left its stamp). Both had a bushelful of frizzy hair — one hennaed, one blued — and both were as gaunt as pterodactyls. Neither was petite, and they were looming into each other at the table's far corner, their body language screaming, 'Prepare to repel boarders!' as they bickered quasi-politely. Some of their tension undoubtedly stemmed from annoyance at being decked out in nearly identical outfits: elegantly inappropriate knee-length black cocktail dresses (no décolletage, mercifully) straight from Saks Fifth Avenue or its ilk if the dazzle of jewelry around every encircleable part of their upper bodies was any indicator. Even Shopping Channel junk in that quantity would have napalmed my bank account.

As is the proper order of things, they ignored me when I plunked myself down on Henna Hair's right. I remembered at the last second not to wedge myself too snugly into the shabby 'folding' chair. It was a bottom-feeder, literally. Unlike its more evolved cousins in the lobby, its minimal upholstery forced it to rely on swallowing chunks whole, with no predigestion. Smoosh your terminal self too far into its throat, then forget and lean forward, and *bam!* — you found out what it felt like to be a mouse. I'd seen several tournament rookies doing a telltale bent-over Groucho walk.

The women's social status being equal, they were each firmly seeing to it that the other knew her place in the bridge hierarchy. Steel rang on steel: a Bob-Hamman-was-at-my-birthday-party lunge effortlessly parried by a sneering my-team-beat-Garozzo's; then a breathtaking flurry of regional placings with Lawrence, Soloway; a slashing Marty Bergen *I-should-be-paying-you...*

Too good to tune out, they were draining me like succubi, when a cooling comber of displaced air broke against my right side. I presumed it signified the arrival of our fourth, praise be. Having long since been battered into accepting that tournaments were no place for actual manners, I dredged up my standard game face, punched in the cursory appraisal option, and glanced up.

My game face dissolved into a flustered gawk as steel-gray raptor eyes engulfed me. They probed clinically, catalogued ruthlessly, illuminating the seedy canyons of my emotional underworld, exposing the shameful dark things huddling there. Even (shudder) Sister Dominica's most menopausally withering glare had never prompted such a need to apologize for my existence. Cops would sell their souls for that look if they weren't already convinced they owned it.

The eyes flicked away, and for the second time that day I found myself scrambling to repack the fragments of my worldview around my gooey interior. I was getting used to it, the way a drunk gets used to summary bisection by parking meters.

The eyes had a different but equally devastating effect on the distaff side of the table. The women were lacquered tureens of simmering hormone soup — not *bouillon de Tom Jones*; more substantial, like *crème de Paul Newman*.

His face was breathtakingly ascetic, the flesh shrink-wrapped on his skull as if his genes weren't programmed to dole out enough skin. The square jut of chin, the salients of cheekbones — everywhere that bone or cartilage met skin looked painful, most notably his nose, which projected violently, like the blade of a boomerang someone had whipped through the back of his head. It would have kept him off a plane these days. He obviously lived on adrenaline and maybe nicotine and not much else that was legal. Photosynthesis was out; sunlight wouldn't have left his complexion that sallow. Moonlight either. Still, having the skin tone of Leslie Howard raised in a tobacco kiln didn't seem to deter women over fifty. Its non-Club-Med-ness was accentuated by startlingly black bushy eyebrows too luxuriant to have sprung from his Imax forehead's patina of skin; they had to have been rooted in his sinuses. A blunt widow's peak of less robust blackness expanded into a streamlined mass contoured to his skull and trimmed to Republican Mean Length. Its part, on the side, was inexplicably normal bone-white, a racing stripe. His ear was the dead opposite of cauliflower.

I'd been peripherally aware of the head's transportation — tall, and of course, gaunt — but I bit back a gape when I saw how fabulously he was turned out: a rich black Victorian evening suit complete with frothy white boutonniere and opalescent triangle of pocket handkerchief, ornate silver fob leading to a watch secreted in the vest, and a crisp white shirt with a black silk cravat banding the starched wingtip collar into proper chafing position.

Halloween, I remembered. *Costume.* I'd already encountered the Easter Bunny and the Tooth Fairy, and been partnered by Ronald Reagan two rounds ago — fittingly, I thought, he'd been the dummy — but this was of another order entirely. This specter looked so utterly *right* in it. I couldn't tell if he was supposed to be anyone in particular, but if the Mad Hatter's tea party had included a velociraptor, that would have been my guess. No rental could have done justice to his morphology and cold, elemental elegance, but the problem was that if ever anybody didn't look like a party animal, the type to splurge on a custom-made costume, he was it — a conundrum that added to his disconcerting effect.

Urrk! Lightheaded... Whaaa...?

I wasn't getting enough air... Choking... *again?*— No! *Being* choked. My ancient Fabulous Furry Freak Brothers pullover was strangling me! I all but ripped out its drawstring and filled my lungs, miraculously without vacuuming up the tablecloth — the card trays saved it. My head tilted back and the Grand Central Station hubbub of between-rounds socializing began overriding the roar of my pulse while gray and pink amoebas exited languidly into the ceiling. My ozone-sensitized nostrils stood down from bracing for the burn. I had time for a couple more deep breaths, lamely disguised as yawn stifling, before I came under attack from another source: in a weird display of textile solidarity, my Fruit-of-the-Looms, aided and abetted by my tattered jeans, were working up a magnificent wedgie, choking my other end. There was nothing I could do about that publicly, just grin and not bare it. Adrenaline sweat pickled my hairier parts.

Score one more for Mystery Opponent. Now he had my *clothes* cringing in shame. That I would have been sitting there buck naked if they'd unraveled instead was of minimal consolation. Thrilling, to see my counter-culture badges for what they were — out-of-date sophomoric affectations. No grace period for nostalgia to soften the blow. I had to think this attack of — *ugh* — maturity had been brewing for some time if a guy in a costume — even him — could precipitate it. Why was growing up hard and mostly embarrassing?

Wishing I could teleport to a storage closet, I wearily re-repacked what were now slivers of worldview. I'd escaped being Heimliched, so I could hope my altercation with my wardrobe had been less dramatic than it felt.

Looking back down, I was encouraged to see the women still simmering away, still unaware of my existence, but then I caught the tail end of an impersonally amused look from guess who.

Groan.

Looking around, I was further taken aback by the overt scrutiny trained on our table. Before I could commit *seppuku* with my section-top letter opener, however, I saw what I would have seen right away if my ego's filter wasn't permanently set on high: *he* was the show. People five and six tables away were standing — not instinctive to bridge players — to get a look at him. Even the directors, as jaded a lot as there is, were rubbernecking while they huddled together and washed down sundry prescriptions with glutinous coffee. I assumed their resemblance to Moe, Larry, and Curly was deliberate. If this was the dregs of the attention he'd been getting all evening, it was hard to believe I'd been too preoccupied to notice him or his ripple effect.

He flared his coattails and sat. Despite being a stick figure, he did it with a deft athleticism that made the chair seem to dive under him like a frightened toady, not a lunging predator. When he essayed a polite 'Good evening' in a light baritone mulled with an English accent (the intelligible kind) my last venal hope slunk away: no Truman Capote falsetto.

I nodded dumbly; the women managed not to swoon. Mesmerized, they followed his lead, sleep-pulling their cards from the tray, completely unaware of being finessed out of a chance to inflict their crammed-to-the-legal-gills convention cards on us. A definite windfall, because defending my bare-bones ACBL Standard one — the same as his — against a partner who had undoubtedly eaten several husbands was unthinkable, and if I had feigned ignorance, she'd have seen through me like I was a mound of pineapple jello — quaking, yellow.

Please, no freaky distribution, I implored of whichever deity had drawn the night shift. I reached for the tray, only to discover my arms and hands had spent their down time devolving into flippers. *Great. Five hundred million years of evolution and I'm Chilly Willy's understudy*, I thought with irritated self-pity as I poked uselessly at my cards with my new acquisitions, pushing the tray around like a planchette — although I couldn't help but reflect that flippers would have kept Reese and Schapiro out of a lot of trouble.

Casually the Englishman shot one cuff and extended an index finger to pin the recalcitrant tray so I could pincer the cards out. Lean as his fingers were, they sprouted from lumberjack wrists; the tray became anchored in bedrock. I saw I'd been right about his diet: the finger was heavily nicotine stained. Against his sallow skin the brownish splash looked natural, like a birthmark.

The cards popped free in a slippery flattened bouquet that I hastened to get safely out of sight below the table. I hunched over stiffly and squeezed my locked wrists between my knees. I nodded my abjectly humiliated thanks, eyes down. What next? Incontinence?

My tank of jitter juice should have been dry, no fumes. Who was this guy that he could keep replenishing it? Anger came as a restorative acid riptide countering the groundswell of inadequacy. *Whoever he is, he's on your turf now,* I reminded myself sternly, an honest sentiment that seemed tinged with bravado only because I was using my knees as a card holder. I was good at being my own ministry of propaganda.

Remarkably I had the presence of mind to recognize that being out to lunch meant I had to be the dealer — never seemed to fail — and the tray confirmed it. I had to do something before I was declared legally dead. I could see spades and aces when I looked down my nose, so I mumbled, 'One spade'. LHO (Large Hennaed One) passed before I was finished, partner barked an equally quick 'Two diamonds', and RHO settled things down with a three club bid measured out like a Napoleon brandy. The introduction of a sane tempo put me further in his debt; it triggered a Pavlovian response that saw my Eocene appendages miraculously regain opposable thumbs and sort out:

♠ A Q 8 7 6
♡ J 6 3
♢ A 10 5 4
♣ 7

Goody. No nine-card suit. Plus I hadn't psyched, mumble-worthy though the bid was. I stammered 'Three diamonds'; a normal tone was beyond me. It irked me; clouding minds with my Clintonesque faculty for radiating overweening confidence garnered me more matchpoints than did my haphazard technical acumen. I didn't need to be reminded that the captain of the *Titanic* had possessed similarly-weighted qualifications.

LHO cut me off again with her pass, and partner announced 'Four spades' and folded her cards. Arrived we had. I had no ethical qualms about taking the hint. I only hoped nobody wanted to dispute her judgment. That prompted a belated check on the vulnerability: no red pockets, the dull silver in ours being a song in my heart. RHO passed impassively after an appropriate but nonetheless suspenseful pause, and LHO and I did it as a duet.

Nobody did any annoying scribbling in scorecards, and LHO snapped the ace of clubs grandiloquently onto the coffee-cratered linen. I got to see:

♠ 9 3 2
♡ A K 10 4
♢ Q 9 8 7
♣ 8 4

```
    N
  W   E
    S
```

♠ A Q 8 7 6
♡ J 6 3
♢ A 10 5 4
♣ 7

West	North	East	South
LHO	Blue Hair	Englishman	Me
			1♠
pass	2♢	3♣	3♢
pass	4♠	all pass	

Full marks for her fold. Blue Hair sat revealed as the pirate Bluehair, keelhauler of the lily-livered. Either she was piqued at being robbed of her pet conventions or Marty Bergen had a lot to answer for.

The Englishman quirked a clump of eyebrow. LHO smirked.

After a lingering silence during which my failure to gush my appreciation provoked a deepening glower from across the table, I croaked out a 'Thank you, partner.' Unmollified glowering. 'Small club, please.' RHO followed with the deuce and I avoided revoking. LHO turned her ace over and carefully squared it with the edge of the table before soldiering on with the nine. He followed with the six, and I remembered spades were trumps.

Hmm. Not a lot of values, but no wastage, I conceded, exasperation segueing artlessly into greed. Bluehair ceased to rotate on a spit in Hell's penthouse as my inward vision gravitated eagerly toward a

Halloween | 19 |

familiar cruciform mosaic alive with red-black-white coruscations — synchronized neurological subroutines on the hunt.

Hope he doesn't unblock his spade king was what they treed. A sensible starting point, certainly. To have a realistic shot at ten tricks, I needed the king onside and a 3-2 split, so why not make a virtue of necessity and hope RHO had the doubleton? Dummy's third spade would uglify his options after I cashed the ace and threw him in on the second round; a diamond was the only return that might not be instantly fatal. *Ace and out will make him pout*. Of course the danger would be pretty hard for him to miss; I might as well have a klaxon bellowing, 'Dump it! Dump it!' if I put the ace on the table. Better the first spade should come from the board to take advantage of the ingrained second-hand-low response. And I should finesse before ducking, because it scanned well — *a finesse, a duck, and he'll be stuck.*

Watching him squirm after he was gaffed would be... gratifying. Yes indeedy. Payback.

If brains could salivate, mine did. I trotted over to the ace of hearts with a conscientiously dishonest six — five from her, nine from him — and called for a spade.

Up popped the king like a Hare Krishna at an airport.

Rats. Brain drool is a terrible thing to waste. Who had I been kidding? Had I expected someone who had X-rayed my soul to suddenly exhibit the obtuseness of a pre-war (pick one) French High Command? And he *was* unblocking; LHO had perked up, but mildly, in a jack-third sort of way. With jack-ten-fourth she'd have been venting magma.

He merely radiated serenity. Sharp-edged serenity.

I won the ace with ill grace, noting the Ali thing was getting old. LHO followed with the five.

Now what?

I was loath to abandon a perfectly good plan simply because it was holed at the waterline. It could still work if he had the jack of spades. Or maybe he had the ten and LHO wouldn't know what the hell to do with her jack when I led low towards the nine...

Brain drool buildup. Very dangerous. From out of the shoebox that was filling in for my memory, my wee-brainies injunction reared up and leaned into me like a Parris Island drill instructor. *DO NOT*

COAST! it raved. *NOT HERE! NOT NOW!* I could practically feel the spittle.

Stupid willpower. Now I had to perform something approaching conscious — worse, conscientious — evaluation. I hated coffee, but I'd have mainlined an urn of it right then.

Skewering him with a doubleton spade had been the bee's knees originally, but maybe I was beating a dead bee.

He can't unblock the king of diamonds. Evidently the subroutines were chugging away, stuck in an elegance loop: strip his other spade, then ace and out to the other doubleton king, assuming he had it, which wasn't a given considering how much we were missing. A diamond endplay *guaranteed* he had no safe exit — but wouldn't force-feeding myself into the maw of his diamond holding qualify as Semtex for my wee brainies?

Click. No.

The good news was that he did have the king of diamonds. The bad news was that I *needed* an endplay. My hazy notion that the heart finesse might work was a pipe dream. He had everything. Patently, neither woman thought attitude signaling should be restricted to cardplay, and they were adepts — seventh dans, I estimated. A measly queen to go with her club support and a stray jack or two might not have induced LHO to butt in at the four-level, but it would have merited a commensurate hitch, enough to destroy our contrapuntal harmony. And her lack of interest didn't stem from a shortage of clubs (although she didn't have five, or I wouldn't have been playing at the four-level. Was I over-analyzing this?), because no matter how many professional 'lessons' they had, players like her never quite got over the kitchen-bridge precept (not that she'd ever been in a kitchen other than to instruct/berate the staff) that doubleton ace in partner's suit meant two tricks and a ruff. Her battle with cupidity would have likewise spoiled our closing duet.

Should I try to drop his queen of hearts? He didn't have a plethora of red cards and his nine looked propitious.

Pffft. Shish kebab was what I craved, injunction or no injunction. Dropping his queen would merely discomfit him, not make him my b— ... ah, pasteboard slave.

Before I could wimp out, I cashed the diamond ace.

Small, small, king.

That, I hadn't thought of. I owed my underwear an apology; I'd mistaken horseshoes for a wedgie. *Horoscope horseshoes* came a-rapping, as of someone gently tapping, and I shivered; labored alliteration aside, I was reminded that Christmas should arrive during Halloween only if you're a department store.

However, paranoia was a lot easier to keep at bay when I wasn't being concussed and asphyxiated. My goose bumps retracted and my lungs expanded. Now if only the trump split was as adverti—

Plan C smacked me in the forehead. The trump split didn't matter! If I ran the ten of diamonds now and he trumped, wouldn't he be... skewered? Trading an extra spade loser for no heart loser had style, but it was art for art's sake... unless he *couldn't* ruff! If he was that distributional despite his unadventurousness and LHO was hoarding a trump stack despite her lack of heavy breathing — maybe her meds had kicked in — I could endplay *her*! (Forgive the exclamation marks; I was cooking.) With her four diamonds and her hypothetical four spades, her club support would be third ace, not fourth, because if she had a singleton heart and it hadn't affected her tempo in bidding or leading, I wasn't leaving the building until the tournament committee coughed up a refund. So running diamonds would leave:

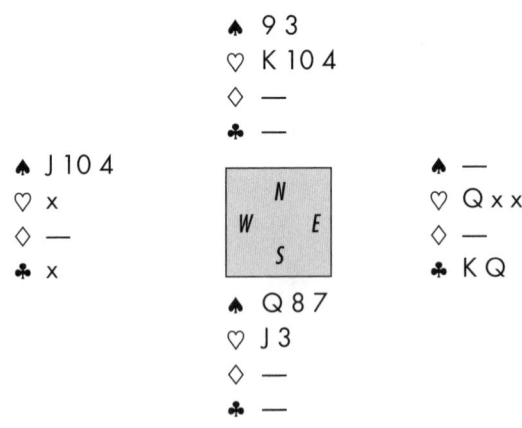

Cash the king of hearts to remove her last one, pass the nine of spades, and voila: instant lemming pudding in a nice bile sauce. A spade return surrendered her trump trick, a club was a ruff-sluff.

Snoopy dance, Snoopy dance.

A pity the skewering was misdirected, but he'd be able to worship it from afar. Had I maybe, just maybe, foreseen it on some level when I banged down the ace of diamonds instead of drawing a second round of trumps? The retelling — and there would be retelling — would be a character test.

I launched the ten of diamonds, steadying myself in its wake with a *que sera, sera* caveat, but boy, was I willing to sign over an organ if he couldn't ruff. Would mounting the trophy for Hand of the Year on my dashboard be ostentatious? LHO's obligatory fumble allowed time for such rumination — and for a twinge of performance anxiety. What if she did have a singleton heart? It would be teeth-grindingly galling to have her ruff the king and give me the bum's rush out of Shangri-la, thence to suck snow forever, all because I couldn't lead a precautionary heart toward the board and then get back to my hand with something other than a trump to run diamonds. The ACBL needed to institute a Fantasy Hand Of The Year trophy for brilliancies that got away, I concluded selflessly. The trophy wouldn't have to be real. A mime could present it. For that matter I could donate it.

Small, small, jack.

Jack? Was he allowed to *do* that in an Individual?

Small spade back.

I dimly recollect fumbling out a small one — flippers again — to let LHO in, in the forlorn hope that she might become pixilated. No dice. She won her ten and pumped back the jack. My bacon unsaved, I played out the string and quietly went down one when his queen of hearts didn't drop. The layout:

Halloween | 23

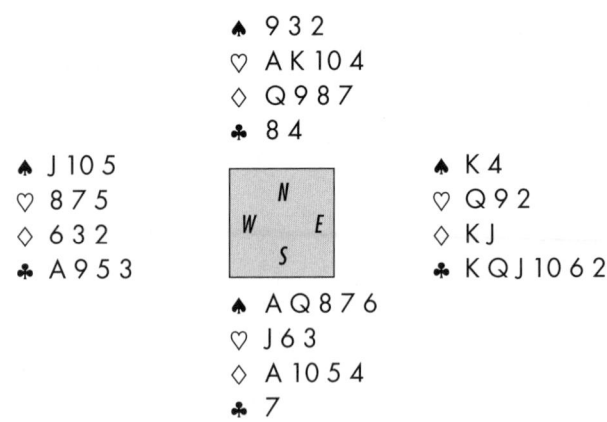

I'd been cooking, all right. As an entrée. His spade, presumed; his diamond, a thunderbolt. Today's theme.

Thunderbolts don't track you down from a clear blue sky, though. You noticed I glossed over a little detail? You weren't alone — and I could feel the spittle this time: YOU DIDN'T PAY ATTENTION TO HER CARDING, PANSY-HEAD! rolled through the corridors of my pansy head. *Not true*, I bridled. She'd played the two of diamonds, then the three. I just hadn't... integrated it. Okay, I'd ignored it once the diamond king propositioned me. I hadn't pondered deeply about her five of spades either. So what? The ACBL hadn't mandated honest count. Yet.

But I couldn't defend the indefensible. She was constantly centering the orange opal in her bangly necklace. She kept her cards a perfect fan, regardless of how many she had, and her turned-over tricks were as exactingly laid out as blocks in the Great Pyramid. Tells of the hopeless anal-retentive. She'd give count in a coma. She couldn't help herself.

That my brainchild had been aborted, and worse, conceived in careless gullibility, was a bitter pill, but kicking (no pun intended) myself around the room wouldn't help, I counseled myself desperately. Hey, hadn't it been a sweet ride? Rocketing high above the mundane ecliptic, propelled by an intoxicating fusion of arithmetic, logic, and psychology: it's why whist died and people don't sleep in their cars for euchre tournaments. So what if I wasn't going to be immortalized?

| 24 | *Bridge Mix*

Bile would have been ambrosia compared to what was festering in my innards. At least I'd bypassed incontinence.

Everyone's cards were back in the tray. Mine were a tad... curly. Odd. Hadn't I calmly restored them after I turned to RHO and, despite the toxic sinkhole sucking my head down my throat, graciously acknowledged his pyrotechnics?

Uh-oh. Warning bells. I wasn't Edgar Kaplan. A Bizarro version immediately unreeled, a grisly trailer featuring me repetitively jamming wadded-up cards into their slot like a deranged Dalek. *Ex-ter-mi-nate! Ex-ter-mi-nate!*

Ouch. That was closer, *maybe* not dead-on, to the me I knew and loved. My fevered flush expanded to a corona, although I could have burst into flames for all the attention I wasn't getting from the two leads of *Whatever Happened to Baby Jane?* They were too busy *oohing* and *ahhing* worshipfully. The object of it occupied himself filling out the ticket. When he was done, Bluehair, the *ooher*, carved out her confirmation on it and backhanded it at a passing caddy, an acned, spindly, prepubescent male with an overwhelming Flock-of-Seagulls hairdo that made him look like the winner of the Most Heavily Inbred category in the Westminster Kennel Club's annual dog-off. He wasn't foolish enough to snag it on the run. He screeched to a halt, ear hoop swinging, and picked the paper gingerly out of the watchet-frosted talons. He got The Glare.

The women rose heavily and, like a handbag drill team, swung the shoulder straps of the heavily bejeweled accessories smartly from one chairback to the other, effectively muzzling the hungry furniture. The fetor of frustrated gastronomic ambition permeated the air as the women then switched places. Even in my fugue state I almost applauded such veteran élan. The Englishman unsteepled patrician fingers from under patrician chin, and I had the momentary impression he *was* going to applaud, but he reached preemptively for the next tray instead. Again he worked his magic; the women groped absently, and mutely, for their cards, adoring eyes glazed. It was getting tedious. As he leaned back he looked directly at me, his gray eyes freighted with a strangely indifferent keenness (sorry, the man gave off a bewildering bandwidth of signals). The corners of his unleavened lips departed minutely from the horizontal in a ghost smile.

My eyebrows collided. Up until that moment, I had considered his jettisoning the diamond king, though impressive, to be nothing more than a can't-lose gambit from a very good player who knew an albatross when he saw it. His almost-smile said differently. It spawned an incredulous certainty that he'd begun laying bricks for my yellow brick road the moment I ruffed the second club, that he'd known everything: her, me, me knowing about her, *everything*.

Deception with a capital 'D'. If I hadn't known he couldn't be associated in any way with my family, I'd have run screaming into the night. From my parents on out to my most distant cousins, all my relatives were obsessive about documenting their existence and just as obsessed with sharing their captured memories at every opportunity. No passing acquaintance escaped their cameras, and in my twenty-odd years of being squeezed between aunts and uncles on couches as photograph albums were passed around and each photo's provenance lovingly detailed, I never saw a face jump out at me the way his would have, no matter how blurry, no matter how young or old. (How old was he anyway? Thirty? Fifty? Drumhead skin doesn't allow for much wrinkling.)

Brrr.

I looked away. Something akin to Stockholm syndrome followed, wherein I tried to rebound with the notion that I should be flattered if he had *expected* me to see the Emerald City — a warm fuzzy that lasted all of a second, since the unavoidable segue was the question of whether he had also expected me to breeze by the crucial warning sign.

Like I did, I lamented. My face went nova, incinerating scads of Who planetoids.

Aside from being another manifestation of the universe's vendetta against me, who *was* this guy?

A discrete glimpse of imperious block letters in green ink squeezed onto his card's masthead billed him as Tobias F. Riendeau. The kind of name usually reserved for a Savings and Loan indictment. It prompted nothing save a conviction that people who affect pointless middle initials should have a finger amputated for each initial. Which Tobias Riendeau did people confuse him with?

That being said, I'd have chewed off a rabid wolverine's scent glands for an opportunity to play against someone of his caliber... if lint hadn't

been the only gray matter in my skull. As it was, I felt overwhelmed.
However, whining like a starving mosquito wasn't going to cut it. That
left but one recourse: into the phone booth that I alone could see, to
emerge as... Duplicate Man! Duplicate Man's alter ego might have been
forced to chow down on snow banks, but Duplicate Man liked his
meat. Duplicate Man lived to crush skulls.

Duplicate Man fanned:

♠ Q 6 4
♡ 9 7 3
♢ 10 9 5
♣ A K 5 2

The auction, them vulnerable:

West	North	East	South
Bluehair	Partner	Englishman	D-Man
	1♢	1♠	1NT
2♠	3♢	3♡	3NT
all pass			

In my new incarnation, my wee brainies were ripe for blowing (more
blowing, technically), and whether the Big Red One (apologies to the
First Infantry) actually had anything became irrelevant as the auction
progressed. When his stab at game, his favorite one, bought the pot,
Duplicate Man, his work done, slipped back to the Fortress of Solip-
sism for beer and pork rinds, leaving me awaiting the dummy with the
equanimity of the slightly crazed. My assets turned out to be:

Halloween | 27

♠ A 2
♡ 10 5 4
♢ A K 8 7 4
♣ 10 6 4

♠ Q 6 4
♡ 9 7 3
♢ 10 9 5
♣ A K 5 2

Not that I could throw stones, but were they sisters?

With no discernible eagerness, Bluehair plopped down the ace of hearts. Who showed up with what in the ensuing heart whirlwind was lost on me as I dithered over whether I could fake an epileptic seizure more convincingly than a stroke. However, the hearts petered out in four rounds, and in the background Duplicate Man belched inspirationally. In fact, as RHO exited with the ten of spades, I noticed with alarm that the ace was singleton and my queen now doubleton; I'd been inspired into pitching spades from *both* hands, torching any hope of a second stopper.

Ruby claws drummed ominously on white cloth. What on earth had I done? Down one or two I could have groveled my way out of. Now, if diamonds weren't my best friend, the opponents could be the ones making three notrump. I had many soft, extractable body parts. *Think!*

There were no darting subroutines this time; counting was a relapse into Sesame Street syndrome, a clumsy pawing at the mental abacus. I wasn't sure it was entirely due to fatigue; the last hand could have planted a seed of triskaidekaphobia. I eventually succeeded in subtracting nine from thirteen — I assumed he hadn't been masterminding the auction with a four-card spade suit and she hadn't raised on a doubleton — to leave him with four minor-suit card cards.

Naturally the possibility of twin sticks of doubleton queen-jacks parachuting to my rescue stuck its tongue in my ear. *Nine* tricks. I didn't furiously backpedal from it either, dumpster-load of horseshoes that it was; the layers of rationalization and repression plastered over the episode in the lobby were severely strained, but holding. Still, it was a ridiculously long shot, and even though crushing skulls was hardly a prime directive when non-elective surgery was in the offing, its negative humiliation index (*I'd* be the one squirming) made it even less attractive.

Of course if cashing the ace of diamonds drew the queen or jack from him, penciled-in scruples might prove academic. Unless I'd been lobotomized in the interim — and Big Red didn't look *that* fidgety — I would be sorely tempted to go with Restricted Choice and finesse LHO for the other honor. Eight tricks that way might look wizardly enough to placate partner. Funny how that had become a priority. Revenge, honor, glory — pretty ephemeral.

Unexpectedly, my adrenal gland gave a squirt of clarity. Wouldn't reeling off five diamonds put the boots to English if he had to hang onto the spade king *and* guard clubs? Nine tricks again and luck with a baseline I could easily limbo under if I felt the need to. My blood, anemic as it was, began to lust. *Ja! Crushen den Englander! Crushen sie!* (*jack*boots?) And while it lusted, my brain ferreted. My adrenal gland seemed to be equipped with an adrenal gland.

If his guarding clubs was to do me any good, it couldn't be by virtue of length; if he had four his partner would then have all the diamonds, too many for me to handle even onside. When he had three, the lousy spots in my hand were no threat, but dummy's fortuitous ten could take over if he had the queen-jack. Nothing inherently squirmable if you're declarer, but to a defender, maddeningly sleazy. Skull pinching.

I had the key now, I thought excitedly: his orphan diamond. It meant...

...meant the climax of *A Fistful of Matchpoints* was all I had. After the opening credits (all me), a lot of blank screen. *Grrr*. Was the diamond an honor? He'd been an honor fountain so far and I hated to buck a trend, even an ersatz one (double *grrr*), so Restricted Choice still tempted me, even if the ever-scary double finesse was superi—

Scratch that. With my proven inability to pixilate, I wasn't going anywhere by double-finessing. As long as Bluehair split her honors somewhere along the line, I'd have to get back to my hand to finesse

Halloween

again, and that would be too much commuting in clubs. My hand would be entryless when the big moment came. Squeeze kaput.

I took a deep breath — something I didn't take for granted any longer — and cashed the ace of diamonds. The queen followed hard on its heels. I accepted it as my due.

Crushen sie!

I remembered to unblock my nine, and Bluehair dropped the two, not a clue (my mistake, Ali never gets old). Too bad we'd changed partners.

Predictably a club toward my ace let English smoothly inject another queen into the mix. I mulled that over, darkly. I had a sudden not-so-uncanny insight that if I went berserk and cashed the king, his jack would appear — and it wouldn't mean a thing. I knew full well he had the chops to sacrifice a sure club trick to conjure up a phantom diamond, and the outlandish elegance of his wardrobe bespoke a fetish compulsive enough to make a Grosvenor gambit, the Holy Grail of elegant grabs, well nigh irresistible. Seeing me go down a lot more if I bought in would be an inconsequential offshoot. To him.

I thrust the creepy digression aside. He wouldn't be getting the chance to use my brain for a squishy soccer ball this time around. However I shilly-shallied (oddly, never a dance craze), I should check to make sure I hadn't done a wishful-thinking miscount. With one diamond left, the ending would be:

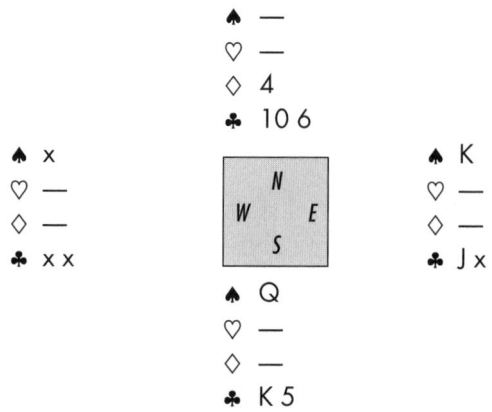

| 30 | *Bridge Mix*

Yep. Buzzard munchies.

Hyperventilating, I led the ten of *yikes*-why-on-earth-did-I-save-*that* diamonds. Bluehair threw a nonchalant six. This was it.

I hesitated. Muffled thumps and yells were coming from a broom closet in the back of my head. What was going on? *Omigod.* He'd returned a spade. Not a club. He hadn't wanted to make me use up an entry prematurely. There was only one way that made sense.

He was awash in doubleton queen-jacks. Breaking up my stupid little squeeze was the last thing he wanted to do. He'd been miles ahead of me again. Waiting for me to get on with my self-immolation was probably as exasperating as having bet on a zombie in the hundred-yard dash.

Without warning, a retooled paranoia struck, arcing down at me and ululating like Tarzan swinging on razor wire. Backing it up came the swampy breath of a fern, the preprandial slobbering of a couch, the sense-memory of actinic light corroding moist membranes. I was caught between worlds again. *What should I do?* I beseeched an indifferently pulsating fluorescent light high above. Finesse and go down on purpose and hope that that would get me off the karmic hook? In essence, lawyering-up against the Supernatural (uh-oh, back to a capital), hoping to beat it on a technicality? Wouldn't that mean it already ruled? I might as well give in, take my nine tricks, and enter the Twilight Zone with my sweet, sweet hide intact.

Several nearby foursomes looked up apprehensively as the light started making bug-zapping sounds, for all the world as if it was trying to answer me. I squelched an hysterical giggle. *What is it, Lassie?*

Fluoresce. Finesse. Phonetic cousins. Why, they were practically interchangeable. Lassie winked at me encouragingly. Winked a lot, actually.

Bite me, Lassie. Ich bin ein bridge player. Ergo, my unregenerate puerile need for validation knew no bounds (no offense). If I was to have a future where leathery wings rustled beneath my bed at night, so be it. Uncle Rodney would have a new drinking buddy — but I would have glory! Squirmy glory on the face of it, and not likely to be immortalized, but *I* would know it was real. I'd be *earning* those nine tricks, no apology necessary, and if I repeated that often enough I might convince myself I wasn't Faust losing his soul via negative billing.

'K-king, please,' I stutter-gushed, my eyes squinching. *He isn't pulling a gun, it's a lousy piece of pasteboard or whatever they make cards from these days.* Regardless, my heart was pounding against my ribs like Cagney railing at the screws. It might as well have been a stomped-on prune for all the blood that was reaching my clammy fingers.

English fanned his cards onto the table, withholding two that he rubbed between thumb and forefinger as he held them up to show me. The minor-suit jacks. 'The rest are yours,' he pronounced in a tone that would have sounded sheepish in anyone else. He dropped them on their brethren.

I was stunned. I hadn't brainstormed myself into another fiasco. In a trance I reached out and fingered his arc of cards like a leper wonderingly stroking new and healthy skin covering his stumps. With nobody around I might have sniffed and licked too, to intensify the memory; it might have to sustain me through a new world order. Partner, in the spirit of the moment, went so far as to not-glower at me.

Witness anew the immortal stage for a glory equal to Thermopylae: (I've been rotating the hands because I was East and it's unnatural to have dummy on the left when you're declarer. We are not communists.)

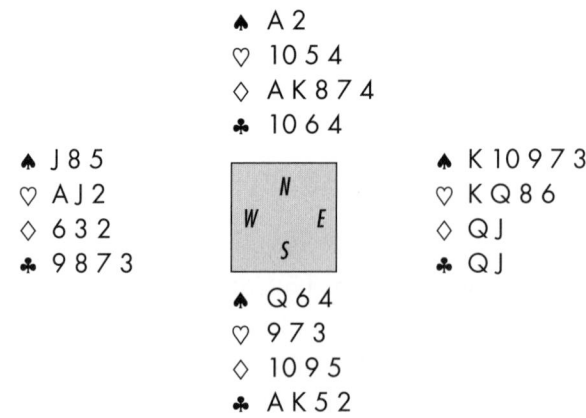

When I was through channeling Rain Man, and my hand, red-faced, came slinking back to me, English did the most extraordinary thing.

He smiled. At me. It stopped short of showing any teeth, ironed itself out quickly, and made me wince at the inside-out flaying his cheeks had to have taken — but it left me propped up in a big comfy wing chair in front of a crackling hearth, enfolded in the toasty softness of a robe the Duke of Windsor would have abdicated for all over again. I wasn't worried about my future any more. Everything would be all right.

Great leapin' lizards! A smile so thin and fleeting shouldn't have been able to do that. But the eyes, ah, those eyes again. There, it lingered. It melted their hard, wintry gray to a quicksilver that seemed to scintillate in delight at my presence. I would have had to be pretty soulless (dare I say, a hollow weenie?) not to respond, and a prodigal grin was tunneling through the detritus of my game face when a counter-sapping operation developed: his next words.

'Hey! My card!'

Those weren't the words. These came when I was alone at the table, and they came in a screechy Bronx accent from close behind me. They echoed in what was now a nearly empty banquet room.

A chair scraped as though the floor was clearing its throat, and once again an apparition entered my life, stage right — a disco version of Michigan J. Frog (the singing one from the Warner Brothers cartoon, for those of you who have a life. Was I being punished for never giving out Halloween candy?). The shiny polyester leisure suit encasing his pudgy body was so blindingly chartreuse it tanned his oversize head a matte version of its color right up past his eyes — thick-lidded eyes, almost all pupil and as big as cue balls. They rendered any eyebrows hypothetical and left only a small dome of hairless scalp that, being in his head's umbra, was its true color — a very pallid but compatible olive. A turtleneck sweater in a plusher allotrope of the suit's headache-inducing fabric cushioned his double chins no neck involved — and a WWE-sized gold chain and medallion. The medallion sported arcane lettering instead of the Playboy bunny, else he would have been sublime.

This time my clothes didn't do the cringing.

Stumpy legs pumping, he scuttled busily up beside the chair beside me while I was queer-eyeing him. The mode of locomotion wasn't froggy, but clown-sized green loafers preserved the illusion. He was

Halloween | 33 |

so short he didn't have to stoop when he draped an arm across the chair's shoulders, yet he *loomed*. An incongruous clean summer scent of gardenias wafted over me as I tried not to think of the crimes against amphibianity I'd been party to in biology class.

Out of nowhere a morbid grade-school giggle-snort threatened. I tried camouflaging my nasal extravaganza as a sneeze by unscrewing an emergency paper napkin out of my back pocket and swiping at my nose. No use hurting his feelings. Or, more truthfully, making him angry. Who knew what his tongue could do? I didn't want to lose an eye now, not after I'd maintained the proper attachment of my body parts at the possible expense of a slide over to the Dark Side.

The charade must have passed muster, because he cheerily informed me, as if he wasn't a near-death experience, 'I'm Toby Riendeau.' His voice was now more appropriately throaty. 'Dey got someone tuh fill in for me, huh? Prob'ly put da kibosh on yoi score, not gettin' ta play 'gainst me.' He chuckled gummily and I stuffed the napkin back in my pocket.

'Blame da elevator,' he continued. 'Haunted, y'ask me. A half-hour I was in dere and nobody wanted tuh use it, nobody hoid me yellin', d'alarm and da phone are a pair'a boinkin' placebos, and den, nice as ya please, it just starts woikin' again, all by itself.' Elongated spatulate fingers, blessedly unwebbed, reclaimed his card. He wrestled a pen (guess what color) from inside his jacket's breast pocket. 'Mind tellin' me da scores?' he asked expansively. An uneven sprinkle of small white teeth peeped at me.

I looked mechanically down at my convention card as a pretext for breaking eye contact. I had to get rid of him. I had to get to the bar.

I went to push myself to my feet, but leaned too heavily on what must have been a purse purge. A clump of slick color brochures glissaded as I tried to keep my balance. I grew bulging cartoon eyes of my own when I lost my battle and buckled into the chair and had to fight to reclaim my hind end from the delighted carnivore's esophagus (a rearguard action, literally). That's when, despite such a massive distraction, I zeroed in on something random, meaningless — to anyone but me. Something I had been primed to see.

Amidst the technicolor chaos brocading the tablecloth, a wedge of his convention card lay scissored between two brochures pimping local Washington-and-Franklin-slept-here-but-not-together-they-weren't-like-that luxury inns. One brochure overlay everything but the 's' of his first name, the inn's name — in apple green — perfectly aligned with his initial and surname. A blank white portion of the other was skewed over the last two letters of his surname. They gave rise to:

Watt's Inn | s F. Riend/

— And the whole collage careened around the inside of my skull like a fuel-injected greyhound, getting leaner, leaner...

Watt'sInnsF.RiendWatt'sInnsF.RiendWatt'sInnsFRiend.

WattsInns FRiend.

HOW? I gasped. *How could it be!* It explained everything, it explained nothing.

Mom is a doctor. As was her father, as are both her sisters, both my sisters, and a mess of cousins. Her family churns them out the way San Marino churns out stamps. Real doctors, not HMO lackeys. It started with her paternal grandfather, whose 1940 *Times* obituary, embalmed in a glassine sleeve in the family Bible, describes 'a man who died as he lived, helping others. On October thirty-first, four days shy of his eighty-eighth birthday, while on his way home after an All Clear, he witnessed the collapse of a burning warehouse on a fire-fighting brigade. No one there will ever forget the sight of him staunching wounds, splinting bones, and salving burns, fishing supplies from the bottomless emergency medical kit which had accompanied him everywhere since the start of hostilities. He was preparing to leave after having supervised the loading of his charges aboard ambulances, when an unmerciful Fate in the form of an overheated chemical storage drum singled him out.'

Mom's maiden name was Watson. Her biblical grandfather is commemorated in my middle names, John Hamish. She remembers asking him why it didn't drive him crazy to have people begin their answer to his every question with 'Elementary'. Or for them to pose elbow-in-the-ribs gems such as 'I lost my virginity. Can your friend find it for me?' He had smiled indulgently at her and answered, 'Constantly

Halloween | 35 |

invoking him, no matter how... unoriginally, keeps him fresh in all our minds. Who wouldn't want that? It reminds me how well and for how long he has entertained me. He's like part of the family, only I will never have to attend his funeral.' I'd always thought that that was stiff-upper-lip for 'I need a death ray'.

I don't know what to think anymore. Not after the Englishman's parting words:

'A fine job, Watson! I'm pleased to see someone in the family still knows when the game's afoot!'

The Pyramid Scheme

'Goggles, mask, earmuffs,' Uncle Bruce warned loudly, reedy voice overriding the whirring of the big fan. I complied, working them up one by one from around my neck with my free hand and fitting them on, keeping the beam of the powerful lantern light trained on the middle of the rectangular tunnel's wall with the other. When we both looked like we belonged on the flight deck of an aircraft carrier, he picked up his trusty pry bar and I stepped back out of his way and slid down the cool stone at my back to sit, knees tented, the light resting on them. Felt good not to stoop, not be envious of people with rickets. The tunnel was large enough to ward off claustrophobia, but annoyingly low for my average height. The ancient Egyptians would not have been high NBA draft picks.

He assumed a home-run-hitter's stance and took aim at the white ellipse on the floor-to-ceiling limestone. The contrasting gloom around us made it seem to glow like a portal to another universe, which, as the fiber-optic camera had revealed, it was: the universe of Egyptian antiquity, where souls set sail for eternity in great stone ocean liners. Through the camera's limited worm eye, this particular stateroom had looked as sumptuous as we dared hope: bundles of spears, a war chariot, tables laden with the usual jars of midnight snacks and what was probably beer or wine — nobody ever seemed to need water in the afterlife — and the people-shaped lumps, heads drooping, of a household retinue sprawled up against the greatest prize of all: a stone sarcophagus sitting like a deep, covered bathtub in the center of the unusually spacious vault. The ceiling was lost in darkness.

Clang, clang, clang went the pry bar. *Zing, zing, zing* went my heartstrings. Dust jetted, but the hurricane-in-a-box we'd set up halfway back along the fifty-foot tunnel sent most of it careening into the tunnel's stygian interior. With ear protectors on — the tunnel's acoustics created phenomenally loud echoes — I could barely hear the fan's loud whirr or the echoing *pocketa-pocketa* of its generator at the tunnel entrance.

Uncle Bruce was a demonic cherub in the reflected light, grunting and batting. The cloth capsule over his nose and mouth only dimpled gently, but sweat flew off him in a horizontal rain. The temperature in the Great Pyramid is a constant comfortable 68 degrees Fahrenheit, but this tomb buried in the West Delta of the Nile wasn't big enough to be immune to the outside world, which is why we usually worked at night. However, near dawn, the ground-penetrating radar had told us we were on to something, and adrenaline had kept us going for the next two hours. That and the fact that it was November the first and I'd made it through another Halloween without incident made the smallest of potatoes out of dealing with ambient temperature and body temperature being synonymous.

A half-dozen muted clangs with the flat of the bent end of what he had just dubbed his 'Egyptologist's scalpel' were sufficient to shatter the limestone facing most of the way up. It crumbled into scree to reveal a brick wall, its mix of light and medium orange making a cheery crossword puzzle in the brightness. He took a break and leaned casually on his scalpel. The back of his trademark long-sleeved red shirt was a Rorschach of sweat stains, but powdered limestone had turned his whole front into a bas-relief of Jack Frost. A pudgy Jack Frost. I clamped the light between my knees and reached into my open backpack beside me and fished out my Leica to document the moment, since the bricks were about to become history. That done, it went back in its case and into the backpack, and he took up the attack again, stabbing and digging at the desiccated mortar that was the last obstacle between us and everlasting fame. And a roomful of really stale air. This was the opposite of good, painstaking archaeology, but we were under the gun. Uncle Bruce alone had suspected there was a royal tomb in this part of the Nile's West Delta, and it was too late to derail the bureaucratic juggernaut driving the West Delta Irrigation Project. Part of Egypt's Big Muddy was slated to be rerouted through here next week.

I kept both hands free in order to use my one talent, making shadow puppets (my Miss America talent, he calls it), to project the bat signal in front of him — his full name, courtesy of oblivious parents, was Bruce Wayne — but it didn't slow him down. He was in great shape, belying his rotund physique. We'd played a furious game of racquetball a month before he'd called to invite me along on this dig, and he'd humiliated my latte-sipping, martini-guzzling, elevator-riding, taxi-transported, thirty-five-year-old ass. So we both knew that when he professed to be getting old and needing help, and wondered if I wanted to take a break from being a stockbroker in a depression, he was actually looking for a way to get me out of the doldrums I've been in, in the years since... the incident. The timing was perfect, and if he didn't mind that my presence was more reclamation project than help, I didn't. Those summers back in my student days when he would shanghai me away from the bridge table to swelter with him near the banks of the Nile were the second-happiest times of my life. Unfortunately, the first were my student days at the bridge table. Still, I learned more about archaeology than I ever could have in a classroom, although I never seriously thought of making a career of it. Too hard to find a decent game out in the field. If only I had known.

He made short work of the dried out mortar, and a few more judicious whacks sent segments of wall tumbling backwards out of sight, kicking up soundless lunar dust blooms. His lanky gray hair was dripping, but his dust mask pumped at the same rate as before. The part of the wall in front of him was now thigh-high with a broad chest-high gap above.

Now that we would be swinging vertically, I leaned the light at an upward angle against my backpack and picked up my own pry bar. Together we chunked methodically at the unsupported bricks near the ceiling. A lunar fog rose as they bombed the floor inside. When the last one bit the dust, we pulled off our protective gear and happily tossed it aside, mopping our brows with already soaked wristbands. The fan on our bare faces was psychological relief if nothing else. I leaned back down to retrieve the light, then dug around in the backpack for the camcorder before I remembered I'd left it to fend for itself in the sandstorm. *Oh well, I can swipe Larry's and fake the grand entrance later. Do the world a favor and tape over his dung beetle documentary.* Larry was one of the grad students Uncle Bruce had sent to Cairo for supplies.

Uncle Bruce insisted I go first, so I bent low and did a slow-motion hurdle over the toothy remainder of the wall. The ancient air cloaked me with a totally unexpected smell, like fruitcake, only very attenuated and mixed with hot copper shavings. I sneezed and he blessed me as he straightened beside me.

'Feels good to be *Homo Erectus*,' he said.

And good to be rich, I fantasized, momentarily pretending this was the nineteenth century and Egypt was a garden of archaeological pillage. Gold, that changeless navigator of the eons, glowed in the shadows, shone in the light. I actually grunted with the effort of yanking myself back to the fame-only, more altruistic present.

I centered the lantern on the court-in-waiting sitting up against their lord and master's resting place, which was sideways to us. The brownish-gray linen tunics hanging off the eight corpses on our side were largely intact, masking their sex, which was fine by me. Nature, not man, had mummified them. Some heads and arms had fallen off, some bodies had keeled over. The morning after of a truly legendary frat party. In contrast the funeral directors had gone to the trouble of mummifying two big, lean dogs. *As is proper*, I thought, remembering Inebrio, my cross-eyed schnauzer, who'd kept me faithful company during long and wakeful nights. They were in mid-stride, trotting after the sarcophagus, the picture of four-thousand-year-old health. They would have been unremarkably generic if they hadn't sported fruit-bat ears.

I slid the bright, wrinkled circle farther along and inhaled sharply as it settled it on a previously unseen figure sitting in profile to us at the coffin's bow. Even after millennia it exhibited the ramrod posture indicative of the military, head still balanced atop the spinal column. A mottled blue-green bronze *khopesh*, the sickle-like scimitar that was the status weapon of infantry and cavalry alike, lay ready to hand on the floor beside him. Even with his soft tissue shriveled and blackened, you could tell his muscle mass had been impressive. And he was big, the kind of big that loan sharks send around to help with your bookkeeping. In a rare honor, a *uraeus*, the royal hooded-cobra headdress, covered his head. Other than that, if you freshened him up and plunked him down on the Riviera, he wouldn't have attracted any attention other than lust, since Egyptian military garb was pretty much a kilt and sandals.

I stepped toward him and took a closer look at his lap, where the linen was splotched black, and I choked, almost literally, on my flippancy. Jaggedness marked his belly. The blackness was a dried pancake of blood and intestines. His right hand, curled in his lap, held a dagger. Realizing the implication, I switched the light back to his companions and saw the yawning lips in their necks. He had slit their throats — and they had probably been willing — then opened his own belly in a final tribute. Time didn't dilute the horror of such devotion to their gods.

'Point it to my left,' my uncle said, breaking the spell, his voice husky. Some things you never get used to. I swiveled the light to illuminate a stark white plinth, hip-height, that had also been out of the camera's line of sight. A vertical slab on top — think Flintstones' computer monitor — displayed large lines of hieroglyphs beneath a very fine layer of dust. We moved closer, unconsciously sidling the five feet or so, and my uncle peered at the message out of time. He read fluidly: 'Stranger, do the opposite of what you intend and you may return to your life.' It was rather polite, kind of cryptic, but you just knew it was threatening a mummy infestation. It reactivated my almost forgotten aortic chill, the one that was the main reason I'd become a reclamation project.

'Are you sure it doesn't say, "Employees must wash hands"?' I forced out between clenched teeth, not fooling him a bit. I'd told him the story.

Without warning, everything suddenly went strange — well, stranger. My surroundings got wavy and distorted, like I was underwater; then my inner ear betrayed me and I staggered. The light jigged, played over the guardian, began strobing... and blinked out. It didn't fail — it disappeared from my hands. Electric glare was replaced by flickering torchlight...

...and the guardian drew one leg under himself. Then the other. He rose with eerie, wavering grace, like a cobra from a snake-charmer's basket, dead leathery tissue of his trunk, arms, and legs fleshing into golden bronze. The head... did something else. The wavering stopped. He turned toward me.

Jackal-headed Anubis stood before me. The coldness of interstellar space radiated from eyeholes in the feral, night-black head. I fought the urge to fall to my knees in terror and worship away the ancient malevolence directed at me. My heart gnawed frantically at my spine, trying to save itself. It almost made it through before I blacked out.

In retrospect, very funny. Especially when, as now, Anubis's fearsome fanged snout opened and this came out: 'I haven't had any decent cards since Rameses turfed the Jews,' his thin, scratchy voice whined at us in familiar complaint. 'What's *that* about?'

His features were squinched in self-pity because he knew he was only talking at himself. His incongruously human body sagged forward on folded arms to lean on the smooth mosaic of mystical symbols rimming the lambent gold of the table separating us. The table was about four cubits across, to show you how well I've adapted. By law Anubis had to look like the renderings of him on temple walls, but when his Nubian (what else) features were animated, his oily, ingratiating manner reminded me of my oldest sister's husband, whom we affectionately referred to as Jerknuts. Jerknuts was a Hollywood agent, but with Pauly Shore as his star client, he mostly sold used cars.

I banged my knee on the outswept wing of one of the twin golden falcon effigies that pillared the table between them, but of course I didn't feel any pain. There was never any pain. Bruising either. I gave my knee another smack just because I could... And because I really, really wanted to wake up. When my dream-self had first found itself seated, alone, at a golden table just like this one, I'd only been monumentally grateful for the escape from a terrifying hallucination. *You really outdid yourself that time*, I congratulated myself bitterly. This time, though, there was no soul-destroying doubt about what was going on: I had that back-of-the-brain awareness I was dreaming — the ability that children don't have and desperately need — and I knew that a combination of heatstroke, bad air, and excitement accounted for the momentary hallucination preceding my blackout (sounds much better than faint). I knew I was passed out on the burial-chamber floor.

Nevertheless, when I'd looked around and seen a wondrous panorama of a pristine pyramid and magically restored monoliths and edifices blazing from a verdant lushness parted by several wide, brick thoroughfares, dream logic compartmentalized my previous existence, tucked it out of sight, and made my surroundings seem a perfectly natural place to be. It was, paradoxically enough, like waking from a nightmare to find myself in the comforting familiarity of my own bedroom, surreal as that bedroom was.

Off in the distance soft green clouds of papyrus enrobed a wide stretch of open water that had to be the Nile. Its freshwater tang smelled a lot fresher than I was used to. The papyrus undulated lazily in a breeze I was not party to and the sun was a radiant circle woven into a large white canopy halfheartedly shading me. A broad transverse avenue lined with two-storey granaries, their brightly colored distinctive barrel vaults making the conjoined units look like an open carton of giant Easter eggs, served as a backdrop for a bizarre threesome (not that kind) chatting casually under a date palm — the plant kingdom's Sideshow Bob — about fifty feet away. One of the trio, a man, was leaf-lettuce green. He was talking to a tall, regal milf with a humongous Betty Page hairdo that even my oblivious male eye recognized as a wig. All I could see of their companion was a pair of legs; I hoped there was more.

As if in response to my curiosity, the trio began heading toward me. I felt no consternation, only curiosity. The man seemed to *prowl* across the manicured grass, *a la* Yul Brynner. He wore the *atef* crown, the one that looks like a bowling pin with two big blue feathers stuck to it, so he could only have been Osiris, lord of the underworld.

Anubis's father. That meant the middle-aged woman with her arm resting on his proffered forearm was almost certainly Isis, goddess of magic, giver of life. Osiris's sister, and wife, and stepmother of Anubis. (It's complicated and has the makings of a very creepy sitcom.) They were dressed in the classic white linen tunics suited to hot weather, and heat duly shimmered above the sand, but I neither felt it nor felt sweaty. In fact my short-sleeved cotton shirt and lightweight twill pants, Kodiaks, and most importantly, my Fruit-of-the-Looms, were fresh and dry, which was at the other end of the spectrum from where they'd started.

They parted as they neared, and to my surprise their companion turned out to be a completely unthreatening Anubis slouching along behind them like any teenager who didn't much want to be seen with his parents. This incarnation of him was bronzed, but physically unprepossessing, slender, and not overly tall. Anubis Lite. When they pulled out the three woven bulrush chairs spaced around the golden oval and sat, Isis opposite me, it seemed like the most natural thing in the world — or wherever. This was some dream, I marveled. Isis deftly unfolded a white square of linen wrapped around a small packet lying in front of her to reveal a royal-blue deck of cards.

'My deal,' Isis said peremptorily, and I was home.

Myriad bracelets clanked, gold rings flashed, and a silver amulet swayed as she leaned forward to dole out the cards. Osiris removed his crown and placed it beside him on the table. No hat-head for him; the bare scalp above his graven features gleamed. It was as bronzed as the rest of him, without the royal equivalent of a farmer's tan.

I picked up my first card and it broke in half. Papyrus. I wondered if this was going to be one of those embarrassment dreams. It drew no reaction, however, and I was more delicate with the rest. I copied everyone else's method of leaning incoming cards against an open hand and sorting them before scooping them up and fanning them. The other half of the broken card I nonchalantly slid into my lap.

The suits were recognizable, ankhs being clubs and hearts being grisly. The face cards were a little mysterious at first glance, but I guessed the godly pecking order would mean the golden chariot carrying Ra was an ace, while the king, queen, and jack were at the table with me. A weird sort of ego boost *that* had to be. The ACBL is missing out on a lucrative sponsorship deal there; I'm sure Donald Trump feels he isn't omnipresent enough.

This was Isis's handiwork:

♠ 6 5 (broken) 4 3 2
♥ —
♦ A K Q 7 4 2
♣ 9 6

She passed with a studiously bored tone. Osiris rumbled one spade in a voice that would have done a creditable job of *Ol' Man River*. I didn't waste my breath opposite a passed hand. Anubis jumped to three spades — I didn't ask — and Isis came in with four hearts. *Eeek*.

If I was actually in hell, I was going to find out now. I breathed again when Osiris bid game confidently, not that I could have pictured him doing it any other way.

Even in a dream and even with a potentially devastating pump suit, doubling the god of death didn't seem prudent. I passed without openly drooling. The others let the contract lie and I was about to pull out the ace of diamonds to do God's work, when I felt something tugging at my awareness.

The first part of the tomb inscription. *Do the opposite of what you intend, eh* (Canadian translation). *I've been here before*, I mused without trepidation; I knew it was only my subconscious using a different context to grapple with the hag that had been riding me all these years. This time, though, the Message from Beyond was dream-softened from an ominous "No Trespassing" sign into something approaching friendly advice, and though my normal reaction to any and all advice was to bite the head off the advice giver and ignore it, my affinity for the perverse (the breathtaking abdication of all reason, if you prefer) had always been too strong for my own good. The tugging was insistent too, like a five-year-old's passing a candy counter — and I'd always been putty in the hands of my nieces' and nephews' whims. *All right, all right, it's a friggin' dream, I'll do it*, I acquiesced. *Who knows? Going down a kinder, gentler rabbit hole might even be instructive.* I was certainly a happy drunk in this dream.

The pertinent question then became what *was* the last thing I wanted to do? Obviously, try for a ruff. Hard to picture *that* resulting in Messages from Beyond 2: Me 0. Which was probably the point.

I hadn't brainwashed myself so thoroughly that I didn't feel a twist of trepidation as I put my fourth-best diamond on the table. Anubis slopped the dummy down on the lustrous gold, which occasioned a stern paternal look, and he did an exasperated tidy-up, complete with melodramatic eye-rolling.

I couldn't help but grimace when I saw:

♠ Q 10 8
♥ A J 6 5
♦ 10 5 3
♣ A 7 5

♠ 6 5 4 3 2
♥ —
♦ A K Q 7 4 2
♣ 9 6

West	North	East	South
Anubis	Isis	Osiris	Me
	pass	1♠	pass
3♠	4♥	4♠	all pass

Three small diamonds. I could have pumped him like he was light sweet crude. I was really sailing against the wind on this one. *Gonna be some 'splainin' to do*, I thought, suddenly remembering bridge wasn't played in a vacuum, even if the vacuum was in my head. Good thing Isis was the *giver* of life. I stole a quick look at her. Anthracite eyes regarded me coolly from within her malachite cat's-eye makeup before she curled the fingers of her free hand and idly inspected nails the same color as her makeup. I didn't sense an Earth Mother vibe. This dream could turn ugly. I was having second thoughts about exploring this particular rabbit hole.

Anubis pushed out a small one, unbidden, and Isis covered with — drumroll as I now deeply regretted my little experiment in error — the jack. Dear little rectangular Anubis. I wasn't going to be mummified alive. However, my audition for court fool was still in progress, because Osiris showed in. Its outcome was in Isis's hands. Her long nails clicked against the table as she slowly and thoughtfully gathered in her unexpected trick.

Diamond. Just return a diamond. Please. Don't think! My vehemence startled me. Any vestiges of a desire to see the — ersatz — supernatural crash and burn had been overridden. Screw the stupid heart ruff; as was the case in real life long ago, when push came to shove I was still a hardcore bridge player. I needed blood.

| 46 | *Bridge Mix*

I sighed as Isis put a small heart on the table. *Oh well... good for her.* When I ruffed declarer's low one, both opponents looked at me like I was the one supplying the weirdness for our little group. Having duly pumped myself, my sense of adventure sated, I trotted out the ace of diamonds — and did a double take when partner pitched a heart. No paying for my sins? Was I myself now a god?

I harvested my diamonds and switched benignly to a club. 'Drawing trumps, claiming,' announced Osiris resignedly, facing his hand. I regarded it intently for a moment — as did Isis, who then regarded me with rounded eyes but said nothing — then was careful to throw my cards in, retrieved half included, face down. Isis did the same; I was apparently still sparing myself an embarrassment dream. No humiliating hilarity over how the new court fool had just performed a Sylvia:

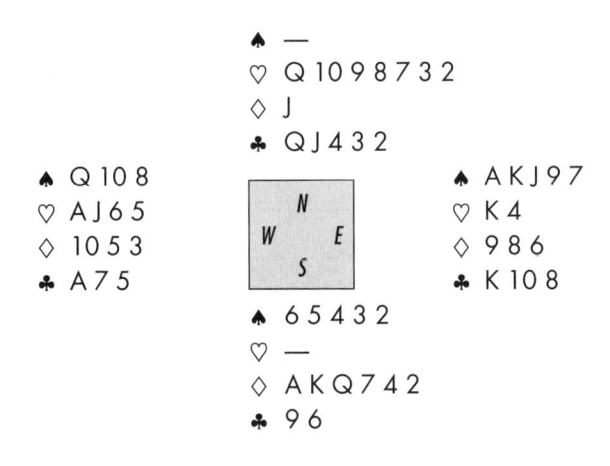

```
             ♠ —
             ♡ Q 10 9 8 7 3 2
             ♢ J
             ♣ Q J 4 3 2
♠ Q 10 8                      ♠ A K J 9 7
♡ A J 6 5         N           ♡ K 4
♢ 10 5 3       W     E        ♢ 9 8 6
♣ A 7 5           S           ♣ K 10 8
             ♠ 6 5 4 3 2
             ♡ —
             ♢ A K Q 7 4 2
             ♣ 9 6
```

Do you see what happens if you foolishly start with a high diamond? There goes your ruff and there goes the defense. If you cash all of them, dummy prevents the pump, and the count is rectified for your partner to be routinely squeezed in hearts and clubs. Not cashing all of them merely means a slower death for partner no matter what you switch to. Declarer has but to keep his wits about him after the shock of the trump break — and Osiris was a god — and run trumps. Isis has to keep too many hearts to leave her with sufficient clubs to cash after declarer unblocks his heart king and throws her in with a club to contemplate her fate. Heck, declarer can simplify things by leading diamonds himself to rectify the count before drawing trumps; you can't do him any harm.

Nice work, subconscious me, I had to say. It had unearthed a long-buried deal from some book or column and paired it brilliantly with a coincidentally appropriate incident from minutes ago, then persisted in putting on its as-far-as-you-can-get-off-Broadway revival of Halloween. Of course *any* opening lead other than a high diamond can prevent whatever shenanigans declarer attempts, but those were also ludicrous enough to fit in seamlessly as understudies. *Kind of a pity about the Message being a sham, though; I might have gotten my life back.*

I wasn't getting it back anytime soon, either. For the rest of that subjective day and into the night, I vicariously (if that's the right word) immersed myself in a bridge orgy powered by my pent-up passion for the game let loose at long last. It was one of those rare dreams that are so real you take hours to disengage from it after you wake up and even then you still have a lingering suspicion you can fly or become invisible if you just concentrate hard enough. I knew again the satisfaction of guessing a queen, finding a killing lead, and sussing out a difficult lie of the cards. It wasn't all frankincense and myrrh either; I blew defenses, miscounted once, misguessed queens — not often enough to weigh me down, just enough to make the good stuff more meaningful. I also became more and more impressed with my subconscious's inventiveness in all areas, not just technical virtuosity. The background clicking of insects, trilling of birds, and the dry licking of breezes against my skin as they wafted the scents of exotic oils and flowers up into my parched nostrils all combined to create a sensurround home theater from the twenty-third century (A.D.). My opponents, keen and inventive as they were, were also invested with sufficient personality that we could develop a degree of camaraderie. Banter took place, which was at once enjoyable and weird, especially with Anubis. I could of course read the nuances of his unhuman expressions, since he was my construct, but exchanges with him were still weirder than with the others; I felt like Doctor Dolittle on the island of Doctor Moreau.

When the next night fell, I started thinking coma. Maybe a chunk of something had fallen on me; maybe I'd sprung some long-dormant surprise for grave-robbers. However, in my floaty, unanchored state, I was simply pleased by my reasoning, unworried by its ramifications.

Another dawn broke and I was in the grip of the horribly familiar sensation of uncertainty about all this being a product of my subconscious. Why was I able to recall so many deals and how their play went? They weren't the vague, non-specific impressions of having been played that turn to vapor when you try to summon them. And my analysis was, well... analytical, not the airhead logic that is the hallmark of dreams. Elapsed time on my unpawned Rolex (better days, better days) was always in synch with what would have been real-time deal durations — as dummy, I often did nothing but watch the second-hand's sweep like a hawk, and time dragged on exactly the same as it always does when you're dummy (I *know* I'm not the only one). I could no longer rationalize that I was running on dream time, when your brain jump-cuts all over the place and the gaps just sort of get backfilled, the way you extrapolate motion between movie frames.

After a hundred subjective days and nights, I still hadn't gotten my life back — no more Messages either — but any concomitant worry had long since devolved into what would have been weary, slogging acceptance if I had been doing anything else, sex included. For bridge, my enthusiasm was still alive, if severely diluted. What made my situation bearable, kept the aortic chill at bay, was that I was constantly improving. The hands weren't leftovers from fifteen years before resurfacing either. I was better than I'd ever been. You can't get that way by dreaming about it, else nobody on *American Idol* would suck. I didn't sleep or get tired, but since no one dreams they're asleep — defeats the purpose — that didn't prove anything one way or the other. I was never hungry or thirsty, so I didn't perform the messier bodily functions; my hair and nails stayed in stasis, and my clothes were still unwrinkled, still operating-room clean. All I did was make up a fourth for whoever was around, and there were plenty who had the hunger. That part was a lot like university.

Maybe I had misinterpreted my back-of-the-brain conviction that I was dreaming; maybe it had only been telling me that this, whatever it was, wasn't real.

'Any wonder I tried to deep-six him?' Akhenaton, on my right, stage-whispered, rolling his eyes toward still-muttering Anubis, bringing me back to day three-hundred-and-something — I'd given up keeping track — of hoping to wake up, or pop back into my own

The Pyramid Scheme | 49 |

dimension, or serve my time in purgatory before joining the heavenly Reisinger, or whatever. He was dipping a sharpened reed in a palette in order to scratch my side's non-vulnerable game on a papyrus scroll. Conflicting shadows from wall sconces worked the room like bustling waiters. The game moved inside at night, usually into a relatively cozy apartment in some pharaoh or other's palace, out of deference to the sensibilities of the defunct monarchs, who were the only ones besides me who knew what a shiver even felt like. At Anubis's side, a glowing brazier in the shape of a standing ibis warmed his elbow.

'Good thing playing the ponies covers my losses at this stupid game,' grumbled Ra, the living face-card, on my left. We played for 'souls', and this was the standard hundred-soul-a-point game. I estimated I was up around nine hundred thousand of them, but don't ask me what one looks like; I'd never seen any actually change hands. Anubis claimed to have Hitler's in a canopus jar, said he wouldn't trade it for a hundred Enron executives. I'd told him I knew some pensioners who might have a different valuation.

I suppose Ra had been brighter when people believed in him. He's like everybody here; they mostly just carry on, like retirees who hang around the office or factory. He and his simple white tunic were glowing steadily, evening out the flickering torchlight. It was easier on the eyes when he was here, but I kept my sunglasses handy; when he got excited, he could still be quite the tanning salon. Previous exposure had upgraded my tan to somewhere between George Hamilton and a blackface minstrel. Tanning and breathing, my least and my most favorite pastimes, were some of the few body functions that worked. I still blinked too, though that was habit; I could have held my eyelids open all day without my eyes filming over.

It was just after sunset, or as Ra regally refers to it, "quittin' time". Time was, he had to work a twenty-four hour shift, but now he's cut back, no longer riding through the Underworld at night. Somebody else would have to cut in soon so he could have his beloved nap, something I was sure he only did on principle; nobody else needed one and he never seemed any less glowy as the rubbers mounted. For a sun god, he wasn't very bright. Take that either way.

Thor came stomping in, *uber*jock to the *n*th, long blond locks flowing from underneath the magnificent winged war helmet that covered most of his face. He was fortunate; poor Mercury was condemned to wear the gay helm forced on him ever since it gained popularity in medieval paintings. Ra's reflection in its mirror brightness parodied a light bulb continually going off in his head, and I do mean parodied; if his dad hadn't given him the thunder gig, he'd have been keeping his brother Heimdall company in the make-work project of guarding the Bifrost bridge over to Asgard. As if a boatload of Haitian refugees was going to show up to blockbust the place. An equally fallacious fire in the belly reflected from the burnished ebony leather of his cuirass.

I'd gotten used to seeing my long-ago nemesis in 3-D by now. This Love Boat for has-been deities wasn't limited to Egyptians, though they did have seniority.

'You working this week?' asked Akhenaton, not looking up from the labor-intensive job of dealing the fragile cards. The Egyptians are such traditionalists; everyone else uses Kem, but, defect or virtue, it's hard to quibble with what sustained their civilization for ten times the British empire's tenure. Shuffling papyrus was like shuffling potato chips, and since gods have seldom been noted for their patience, cards got thrown in the garbage when a deal was over. An apparently inexhaustible supply of them, individually wrapped in linen, was always stacked on a nearby trestle.

Akhenaton had been Pharaoh, so union rules made him a god, but his transition to godhood hadn't involved an improvement in his physique. He was still a weird-looking dude for someone who was — had been — human. Based on the few and very unidealized statues extant, it has been speculated he had Marfan syndrome, which causes a freakishly elongated skull and wide hips with a comparably female top story. He could have sprung from the loins of Bea Arthur if she had mated with the *Alien* monster. He couldn't do much about disguising his figure, but he rarely took off his uraeus.

'Got a drive-by in Atlantic City,' Thor growled, doffing his helmet and placing it on a golden washstand in the corner before bending over to splash water on his visage — 'face' didn't do it justice — and, not coincidentally, giving us a chance to admire those selfsame Fabio features. Anubis seemed to be admiring a trifle too intently. When he was done toweling off, he opened his locker (read amazingly bejeweled silver armoire) beside the washstand and pulled out his Ithaca 12-gauge over-and-under with the beautiful walnut stock ('Walls have nuts?' was his latest favorite joke. Almost all Vikings have a five-year-old's sense of humor.) and leaned it against the wall. Next came his fire-engine-red ammunition pouch, which he looped over his shoulder, cross-body. It was monogrammed to boot, emeralds on the flap forming an 'X' and a vertical arrow, which were the runes — or as Loki put it, 'Norse code' — for GT (God of Thunder). Gucci could rest easy. He picked the gun up and broke it open to pop in a couple of shells, cradling it in one tanned, brawny arm. Scaring the bejesus out of children and golfers was supposed to be done, again by law, with Mjollnir, his hammer, but when you were as pretty as he was you could get away with a lot. Still, he kept his stuff over here so as not to aggravate Odin by flaunting it.

'Don't do anything I would,' he threw over his shoulder as he departed through the archway, his bootfalls echoing in the great hallway beyond.

I thanked Akh, sincerely, for his laborious dealing, but pointed out it was my deal. He was very absent-minded, always thought it was his. We let him. Mummification should not have included removing the brain. He nodded without complaint.

This was my stunt double's effort:

♠ 7 2
♡ A Q 5 3
♢ A
♣ A K 8 5 4 3

Wow. Vulnerable, yet. I could never have done this for myself. I bid one club, Ra glowed half a watt brighter — talk about a tell — and Anubis jumped to three clubs, which I'd found out was forcing in Egyptian Standard. I took it with a grain of salt, since he has no fear of going to hell, and Akhenaton chimed in with a reasonably paused three hearts. Defending might have proved lucrative, but who would? I bid six clubs. Ra passed bemusedly, partner with suspicious haste, and Akhenaton stone-facedly. The stone-facedly part was comforting.

After some thought, Ra picked out the ten of diamonds with his beak (did I mention he had the head of a falcon? I've gotten so used to that sort of thing) and dropped it face-up. Rather handy to have a third hand. Anubis plunked his cards down in orderly files. He didn't bother channeling James Dean if Dad wasn't around.

These were my combined assets:

♠ A J
♡ 9 6 4
♢ J 3
♣ Q J 10 9 7 6

```
    N
W       E
    S
```

♠ 7 2
♡ A Q 5 3
♢ A
♣ A K 8 5 4 3

West	North	East	South
Ra	Anubis	Akhenaton	Me
			1♣
pass	3♣	3♡	6♣
all pass			

Yechh. Three small hearts. Right high card, wrong distribution. I checked again, but no, one of them wasn't a diamond. I played small; small, ace. I extracted the lone trump — Akh had it — with the queen and finessed the heart. Akh played the ten and Ra unexpectedly showed in with the eight. Peculiar. Another trump to dummy, opponents pitching crap I barely noticed, let me ruff the jack of diamonds with the trump ace as Akh covered with the queen. Did I have a plan? No, I was on automatic pilot, playing quickly to simulate being decisive. I've found acting decisive when the outcome looks hopeless makes me feel like I'm in control, the same way the physiological act of smiling can actually cheer you up. But *was* there any way out of this? And had I already — there were obvious disadvantages to being slapdash — blown it?

Well, Akh's vulnerable sandwich-seat free bid at the three-level with a less than robust five-card suit would seem to require he at least

The Pyramid Scheme | 53 |

have the missing high cards. What if I ran all my tricks at him? That would give me:

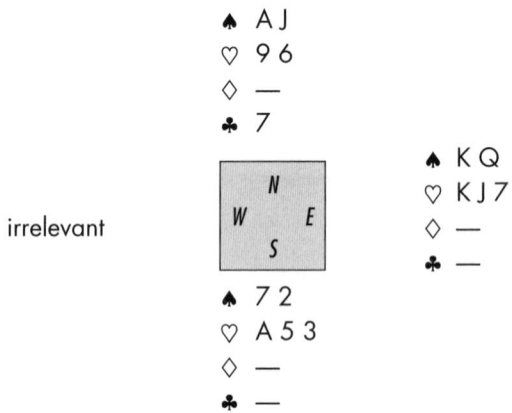

	♠ A J ♥ 9 6 ♦ — ♣ 7	
irrelevant	N W E S	♠ K Q ♥ K J 7 ♦ — ♣ —
	♠ 7 2 ♥ A 5 3 ♦ — ♣ —	

E-e-xcellent (there's some Mr. Burns in all of us). The last club pickles him into pitching an instantly fatal spade or a belatedly fatal heart. With the latter, I duck a heart. Bingo. More souls would be mine.

From out of nowhere, the tomb inscription was back. With a vengeance. No gently insistent tugging this time; it was a gay longshoreman with a hand clamped on my crotch. *What? What?* I squeaked internally, frantically casting about for something to appease it, some way to—

Ah. Akh's bidding. Ra's mini-glow.

The pressure eased.

If it had hit me this viscerally the first time around, I would have been terrified no matter what its presumed origin. By now I was so inured to the surreal that the extra forcefulness was surprisingly easy to shrug off. More of the inexplicable didn't concern me as much as did the possibility I might finally have reached my bridge saturation point: How had I not taken my opponents' quirks into account? This place was going to be unbearable if I let myself slide like that.

Thus prompted, I looked at Akh with fresh eyes. Akh, who's down about a billion souls. Who seems compelled to go for numbers. And then there was Ra's mini-glow. He can control it to a large extent, but he'd apparently been caught off guard.

I cashed the ace of clubs and led low over to the ten. Crunch time. I mentally fingered another trump, looked at Ra. He had a void and a singleton, a perfectly valid reason to perk up with a yarborough. Still...

I changed chariots in midstream. I cashed the ace of spades, raked the trick in, then — *quickly, quickly, don't falter, don't show fear* — led the jack. Akh played small — *Yes!* — and Ra won the king. He dimmed in worry at his awkwardly timed entry. He had reason:

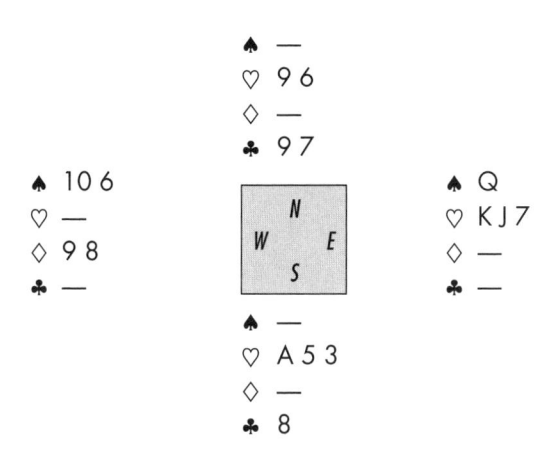

```
                ♠ —
                ♥ 9 6
                ♦ —
                ♣ 9 7
  ♠ 10 6                    ♠ Q
  ♥ —         N             ♥ K J 7
  ♦ 9 8     W   E           ♦ —
  ♣ —         S             ♣ —
                ♠ —
                ♥ A 5 3
                ♦ —
                ♣ 8
```

Reluctantly he returned a spade. Dummy sluffed, I ruffed.

The whole deal, for the completists out there:

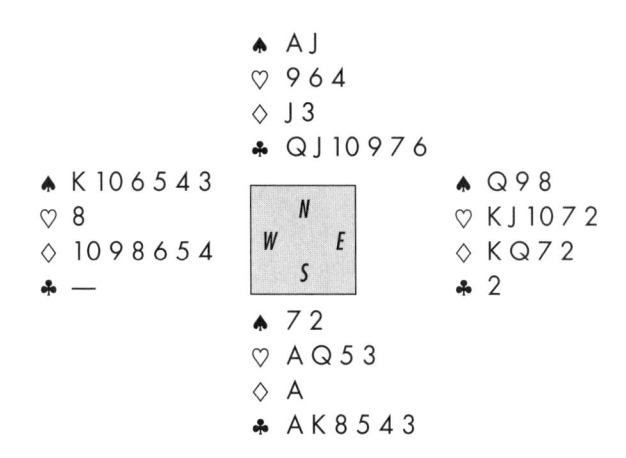

```
                ♠ A J
                ♥ 9 6 4
                ♦ J 3
                ♣ Q J 10 9 7 6
  ♠ K 10 6 5 4 3            ♠ Q 9 8
  ♥ 8           N           ♥ K J 10 7 2
  ♦ 10 9 8 6 5 4  W   E     ♦ K Q 7 2
  ♣ —           S           ♣ 2
                ♠ 7 2
                ♥ A Q 5 3
                ♦ A
                ♣ A K 8 5 4 3
```

The Pyramid Scheme

Recrimination time. Akh's cards flared in the brazier as he reached for a new deck as if nothing had happened, but even Ra noticed I'd made a pretty stupid play if I had the queen of spades. I whipped out my sunglasses. I needed to ask someone if they could score me some suntan lotion.

'Why didn't you cover' he asked acidly, his disposition distinctly un-sunny. Now that they were on equal footing as gods, Akh didn't back down. 'Second hand low,' he replied blandly, knowing how infuriating his lack of self-abasement would be.

Ra snorted, rose majestically, and pointedly ignored his erstwhile partner as he bade each of us goodnight. He turned and swept out of the room, his anger-enhanced wake temporarily annihilating the shadows on the wall he passed. My sunglasses went back in my pocket. My skin was now nearly as dark as Anubis's head.

I didn't join in with Anubis's ribbing over Akh's asleep-at-the-wheel defense; with time to think, I was beginning to stew a bit over how vigorously future Messages might vie for my attention. Which is why my spirits lifted so much when Loki moonwalked majestically through the archway, then followed it up with a few more Michael Jackson moves while belting out his own unrepeatable version of 'Billie Jean'—the tennis player. Hilarious. We all guffawed him his due. What better entrance for the god of mischief? Every day is April Fool's with him. He's my favorite, probably because of our shared sense of humor — off-the-wall, mean, and sometimes Andrew Dice Clay stupid. It was no coincidence his arriving after Thor departed. They are, as Loki put it, 'Oil and water-on-the-brain.' He refers to his brother as the god of blunder.

He appeared as cheerfully evil as ever, a sly, green-eyed Anthony Perkins, and he was the toughest opponent here. In old woodcuts he's medieval dapper, which isn't saying a lot — wool, wool, and more wool, from leggings to serviceable hooded cape. Organic and elfin. Now Marvel and its video-game progeny have amped that into a spawn of the catwalk — a vastly-caped, spandex-clad mass of sculpted muscle in emerald green with a golden Dali-esque fortress of a helmet sprouting slender horns half again as tall as him and hooked forward like the tops of giant question marks. The Norse version of the Riddler. A far more extensive makeover than Thor's.

Rumor had it that Isis and he were a number. I suspected the Egyptians had been glad to see the upstart new gods popping in; they could stop dating within the family. The place had apparently been the Ozarks with gold bathtubs.

Akh got up and minced over to Ra's golden chair, mumbling about changing his luck, and plunked himself down. Ra always sat West because of its personal symbolism. Akh squirmed around uncomfortably; the chair was more a glorified stool with arms, and it could do in even a god's spine after a dozen rubbers.

Loki swung a limber leg over the vacated chair's back with a check-out-these-quads ostentation to sit, slowly bending the leg, the other one folded into his lap, yoga-style, all this to the accompaniment of a hydraulic whine. He may never get over his newly buff persona. Beer fumes suddenly abounded, rich and yeasty, and thickly enough that my eyes would normally have watered. I would have loved to indulge as well, but my one casual experiment with dining early on had tasted like it was in the wrong orifice. Something didn't want me distracted from bridge.

Ra dealt some more, and there I was, Loki on my right, with:

♠ A 3
♡ 7 6
♢ A 10 8 3
♣ A Q J 5 4

Three quick passes went to me. The weak notrump was all the rage, so I started with a somewhat random one diamond. The opponents showed no signs of life as Anubis bid a spade, I replied two clubs, he raised, and I bid a straightforward, perhaps beer-fumed, five. Nobody cared, and Akh led the jack of hearts into:

♠ K Q J 8 5
♥ 5 3
♦ J 5
♣ 10 9 6 2

♠ A 3
♥ 7 6
♦ A 10 8 3
♣ A Q J 5 4

West	North	East	South
Akhenaton	Anubis	Loki	Me
pass	pass	pass	1♦
pass	1♠	pass	2♣
pass	3♣	pass	5♣
all pass			

The jack went to Loki's ace. The queen followed, then the diamond king. I won my ace gloomily. Passed-hand Loki had already showed up with too much to have the club king as well, which meant putting the Rabbi's Rule to the test. I'm not Jewish. I glanced at Akh out of habit, but it was pointless. His features were the usual mask, an asset he'd retained from surviving his reign as one of Egypt's premier shit-disturbers for as long as he did.

Wham! This time, the warning was a cigarette boat going flat out and I was on water skis behind it, getting my arms jerked out of their sockets. *I shall rethink my decision*, I decided posthaste. The boat cut its engines. I slowed and settled. Operant conditioning like this could make an opossum into Garozzo. This time I didn't even *think* about its genesis.

What had I missed? Loki couldn't have the club king; in fact I was surprised he hadn't opened with what he had. He was Asgard's Marty Bergen. On the other hand...

I knew he had at least nine points. He'd showcased them. And he was the Trickster, which I'd learned over the... months?... was not a

PR flack's invention. Why was he solicitously handing me a roadmap? *Hmm.*

I crossed to the spade king and pulled out the ten of clubs. He impassively followed low. I hummed, I hawed — and let the ten ride.

It won. Just as importantly, now that I'd blocked the spades, Akh followed. This was the impossible setup:

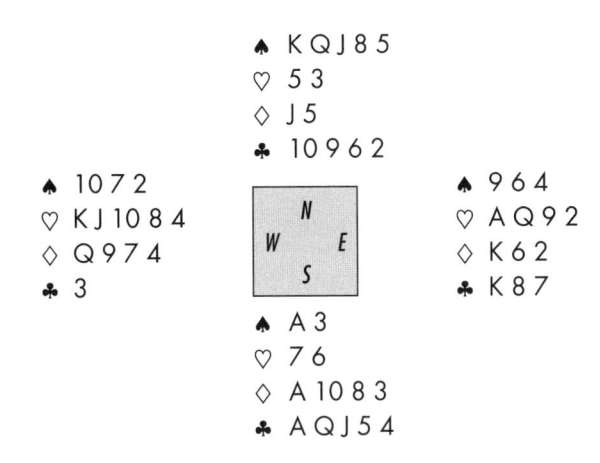

```
                ♠ K Q J 8 5
                ♥ 5 3
                ♦ J 5
                ♣ 10 9 6 2
   ♠ 10 7 2                        ♠ 9 6 4
   ♥ K J 10 8 4    N               ♥ A Q 9 2
   ♦ Q 9 7 4     W   E             ♦ K 6 2
   ♣ 3             S               ♣ K 8 7
                ♠ A 3
                ♥ 7 6
                ♦ A 10 8 3
                ♣ A Q J 5 4
```

Loki's countenance filled with the kind of dark clouds that were Thor's domain. 'Have you been taking lessons from my brother!' he thundered, appropriately. 'How could I have passed with twelve points! I am Loki! I am not Roth!' If I'd had a bed, it would have been short-sheeted for weeks.

I was dying to say, 'You *aren't* low-key,' but it didn't seem like the time. I reluctantly edited myself down to, 'Trickster, baby, you mis-sorted your hand, didn't you.'

More thunderheads roiled across his brow. Abruptly they fragmented, blown apart by a huge chortle of innocent delight that managed to also be disturbingly maniacal. 'And here I thought my carelessness was going to be a blessing and an opportunity to hone the legend that is me!' The last part finished up in a Richard Widmark giggle. It stopped and he looked over — and down — at me. 'You have done well,' he said in a strangely intimate voice. That's when he began to get wavy, distorted. More laughter trumpeted from him, and his already sizeable bulk expanded, growing taller and taller like Jack's beanstalk, reaching towards the forty-foot ceiling. His voice boomed: 'Go now! You have amassed a million souls! You have earned your life back!'

I hate that antiseptic hospital smell. It assailed me now, along with the usual rattle of passing carts in a hallway and the weary chirrup of double-shifting nurses. There was the tap-tap of high heels signifying the passage of a hospital administrator. And a steady beeping near my ear. Against my better judgment, I opened an eye.

A startled Uncle Bruce sitting bolt upright in a slingback chair, craggy face alight, was my reward. He was a vision in heavy argyle and far paler than usual. We weren't in Egypt anymore. He blinked. I blinked.

'Who's patrolling Gotham?' I croaked, rust flaking from my vocal cords.

He wasn't a demonstrative sort, so I was taken aback when he sprang at me, braked at my bedside, and planted his arms on my shoulders and a long, droning kiss on the top of my head.

'I was out *that* long?' I think it came out 'Izowtatlung?' Working my voice box was gutbusting exercise quite aside from the clean and jerk with my eyelid, and I promptly fell asleep. Dreamless sleep.

When my consciousness next coalesced, I was strong enough to crank open both eyelids. This time the gallery consisted of Mom, Dad, Maya, and Anubis... no... no, it was Jerknuts, I realized muzzily and not with as much relief as I would have expected. His skin was ruddy, his features were uncompromisingly Caucasian, but his momentary, unguarded 'What-am-I-doing-here-when-I-could-be-having-fun?' expression corresponded exactly with what I would have expected from the ol' scavenger god. My sister is such a dedicated proctologist she even married an asshole.

Mom took two quick steps and sat sideways on the threadbare bedspread. In a stunning display of affection she covered my malingering — and heavily tanned — hand with hers. Her aristocratic features were more drawn then I remembered, her tight bun of hair more heavily silvered. Her ice-blue eyes glistened uncharacteristically in the fluorescent light. Dad and Maya, androgynously alike with their long gray hair, waited on deck, beaming, ready to swarm me like a basketful of blue-eyed puppies. As usual, Mom took refuge in her clinical mode that had trained a generation of interns. 'You've been... away from us for exactly one year now, dear. You appeared to be in a coma, but your EEG and everything else — heart rate, breathing — indicated you should have been awake and experiencing intense mental activity. And your melanin production' — here she got caught up in the analytical possibilities, eyes momentarily glazing — 'was completely incomprehensible!'

'You were last month's centerfold in the *New England Journal of Medicine*!' Maya chimed in salaciously — for her.

Mom smiled fondly at her firstborn and then regarded me quizzically with what I knew to be gentle concern, but her inborn intensity distilled it into pure Torquemada concentrate. I used to tease her by addressing her formally as 'Mater' whenever she did it. 'I know how weak you are, dear, but if you could blink once for yes, twice for no, I'm dying to know if you have a clue why Bruce would say, "Maybe the supernatural doesn't run on Egyptian Standard Time," when I asked him why he thought you might... come back to us tonight. You know how he loves being enigmatic. But he *insisted* we shouldn't leave at suppertime tonight.'

I stared, comprehending at last. I hadn't made it to the last November the first after all.

'Don't give it a second thought,' she consoled me, when I wasn't forthcoming. 'It was selfish of me to ask. If I were a cat, curiosity would have killed me at birth.' She brightened. 'We brought you a little something, just in case,' she continued cheerfully, actually squeezing my hand. Dad brought the little something out from behind his back. A fluorescent orange plastic jack o' lantern. He set it on the nightstand. 'The candy's a little melted,' he apologized wryly. 'I left it under the car heater.'

'Happy Halloween!' everybody chorused.

Close Encounters of the Unkind

The moon was indeed a ghostly galleon and I was far beneath its keel, being pulled swiftly along the seabed behind the fluorescent reins of my Infiniti's headlights. Furthering the illusion, a westering breeze had set the dark and limitless cornfields on either side of the raised highway waving like beds of kelp. I was racing homeward in an attempt to get there before it got too late for trick-or-treaters — the real ones, not the drunk or stoned high school (apt, very apt) kids who generally came out later and were trying to recapture a childhood they could dimly sense slipping away. Out of fear of repercussions from human and other sources, I never turn off the lights until midnight, so I have to put up with the nostalgia crowd. One time, a boy — if six-three still qualifies — showed up at eleven, wearing a slovenly white T-shirt, pants that started at his knees, and a tie. When my Dutch courage got the better of me and I elbowed aside my teenage nephew, who had 'volunteered' to be the actual candy dispenser that year, to indignantly inquire what the deal was, he condescendingly informed me he was a lawyer. Such impressive chutzpah got him the candy apples without razor blades.

I was coming from, of all things, an afternoon side game at a bridge tournament. Yes, I could do that again, and on Halloween, even. I couldn't face a doorbell yet, but I could face a well-lit roomful of people. Or a roomful of well-lit people, if we're talking midnight games. One step at a time. I'd been gorging on bridge ever since I got out of the hospital after my last… adventure. A year of my life had passed me by — and it had been purgatory, make no mistake — but in truth it had been a happier time than the limbo of the previous fifteen. I at least had been immersed in a pastime I loved. Once it was over, I resolved not to deny myself the same pleasure in real life just because it was inextricably — and inexplicably — entwined with whatever jollies this stupid pagan festival got out of being Godzilla to my Bambi. I could only be glad Christmas hadn't turned on me. I've developed the fatalism of a kamikaze pilot (the downing of the ceremonial *sake* has helped) and I've struggled to leaven it with the meager leftovers of my adolescent *joie de vivre*.

The kamikaze part could have used the *sake* to good effect during the next five minutes, because seemingly from nowhere the sky fissioned into a giant split-screen. The moon was still riding high on my left in a softly phosphorescent impressionist sea spotted with innocent clumps of fuzzy jellyfish while the half on the passenger side billowed with the lightless ink of a million frightened octopuses. Clouds so impenetrable had to be engorged with torrential rain; their constipation couldn't last much longer, and when they let go, being underwater wouldn't be an illusion. The Infiniti was a good car, but it wasn't the *Nautilus*.

A scalloped ribbon of moonlight pewtered the clouds' leading edge, but was being rapidly compressed by changing perspective as the black mass scudded across my windshield... yet the wind hadn't picked up. There should have been a hurricane blowing to change the sky that fast, but the kelp, er, cornfields, were still just tossing and turning fitfully in their sleep. The succession of shimmering dinner forks off in the distance was doing no more than a deliberate Sorcerer's Apprentice march towards me.

'Not liking this,' I said to the Marvin the Martian bobblehead on the dashboard. He nodded in commiseration. I envisioned doing a screeching bootlegger's turn and hightailing it to the hamlet five miles back, though I hadn't watched enough episodes of *The Dukes of Hazzard* to know how, and the town's lone motel was attached to a rundown gas station and looked like the sort of place where the sheets would get up and follow you. Then I remembered how its sputtering fifties red neon sign, an ironically rampant buffalo, had proclaimed in accidental shorthand 'O VACANCY'.

'Screw it,' I said aloud. I was still feeling lucky and reckless from winning the your-name-here-if-you're-dead side game. My pickup partner had dressed like a cowboy and bid like a bucking bronco, but we'd held the cards, and the defenses against our insane contracts had been awesomely inept, propelling us to a 70% game. Barely enough to win, incidentally. Not really bridge, but being able to cruise and get away with it was sweet payback for all those righteous 48% grind-'em-outs.

In short order the moon was eaten and a dimmer switch faded the still-open quarter of the heavens until only starlight remained. My eyes struggled to adjust. The highway was now a very short conveyor belt hurling an endless supply of luminous dashes at me out of the darkness. Not taking my eyes from it lest a corn-moose — or whatever lived out there — tried to commit suicide, I reached down to turn on the radio and fiddled with the dial, looking for the aural equivalent of a baby's soother, but blasts of static from the approaching lightning made music unlistenable. I gave up and did a slow once-through looking for talk shows to keep me company, since static there was generally an improvement. There were far more than was justifiable. I got to hear the lead guitarist of an eighties hair-band explaining, laughably, that they didn't play to sold-out arenas nowadays because 'you have to play clubs to keep it real'; a huckster shouting, 'Got a special day coming? Remember Earl's diamonds! Give a diamond, get a heart!'; a Chicago advertising guru being interviewed on his hometown station, pontificating that 'major contracts can change your fortunes.' *Duh.* 'Proctor and Gamble loved the rapping soap bubble.' The Larry King clone lobbing softballs at him sucked up shamelessly, obviously angling for a career change. I settled gratefully on a broadcast of Orson Welles's classic *War of the Worlds*. A less than tranquil theme for the evening — better than *The Legend of Sleepy Hollow* — but that magnificent voice, rude interruptions included, soothed.

That was when I noticed that one or two of the flashes that were finally beginning to encircle me weren't thin, jagged cracks in the blackness, but iridescent pearly bars. St. Elmo's flashlight? Levity as a defense mechanism had kicked in; I was getting that all-too-familiar 'Oh, no' feeling. 'Liking this less and less,' I confided shakily to Marvin, only to discover he was no longer on the dashboard, but cowering under the passenger seat. Charitably, I assumed the last pothole had been responsible.

A hundred yards off my flank, an express elevator of light grounded, and that's when I really freaked. It was as wide as the road. No roar of static. No clap of thunder.

The speedometer doubled as a blood pressure monitor, its needle arcing past the zenith and down toward the big numbers as I commenced plunging wildly through the night, balloon-eyed and reeling. A half-minute later I was coming up on a large wooden gate guarding a dirt side road over on Marvin's side when the bright doom of Hiroshima suddenly bloomed around it — and the gate vanished. *Hoo-hah.* A nearly simultaneous lightning flash extended my viewing time sufficiently to see there was no smoke, no charred remnants. It was just gone. The radio roared at me. I clicked it off.

'Sweating fiercely,' I announced to the deserted dashboard. I glanced at its clock: 6:40. Thirty minutes from home. An infinity to the safety of midnight. I knew the road was as straight as a hustler's pool cue (too much Damon Runyon as a kid) for the next fifteen miles and I was tempted to dive under the blanket in the back seat and take my chances with cruise control; instead, my foot bore down on the gas pedal and the Infiniti revved to a hundred.

A split-second after I accelerated, one of the ravening beams hurled itself at the pavement right behind my back bumper. *Gulp.* This was getting personal. For no rational reason, I started weaving as much as I dared at Mach 1. *Moan.*

Something was happening in my side mirror. The roiling blackness in it was growing an eye, a mottled red eye. I spared a direct glance — and nearly ended up in the ditch as I beheld the preternatural birth of a great, dully glowing rubescent disc from out of the clouds' placental mass. A heartbeat later, it slid directly overhead, pacing me. My eyes practically crawled out onto my forehead as they tried to look up through the roof window while keeping track of the hurtling highway in front. A shadowy red, like emergency lighting, bathed the car's interior and spilled out into a speeding circle spanning the road from shoulder to shoulder and way out into the cornfields. I cracked and looked straight up just as the disc's navel brightened.

Blinding light. My whole body chewed tinfoil.

A minty formaldehyde odor imposed itself on me. Groggily, I looked at thirteen cards fanned in my unsteady hand. Unsorted, the way I like them. I was seated at one end of a featureless oblong white room awash with brightness from banks of fluorescent lights on the high ceiling. The buzz from a failing ballast in one of them sawed deli-

Bridge Mix

cately on my nerves. The next thing I saw, sitting in a folding chair on the other side of a coffee-cratered square tablecloth, was Anubis — but an Anubis encased in a blindingly chartreuse polyester leisure suit.

'How ya doin', pally,' he greeted me in a croaky Bronx accent. *Gaahh.* Tobias F. Riendeau's off-putting voice, as perfect a complement to the outfit as I remembered. But it was Anubis; something definitively non-human lurked in the bottomless depths of his eyeholes — although now I swore I could see stars in there as well. The black velvet of his snout wrinkled, baring his fangs in his uniquely greasy smile. He was trying for reassuring, and it didn't come naturally. I gave him credit for it. A nightmare trying to reassure me. How bad was that? New reality show: 'I'm a nonentity — get me out of here!' The shiver that ran through me had little to do with the room being on the cool side.

He used one hand to carefully scoop up a palisade of overlapping cards propped up against the back of the arm resting on the table. He fanned them extra carefully too, elbows triangled on the table. I fingered mine for confirmation: papyrus. Before I could try to come to terms with any of this, a familiar *basso profundo* voice beside me intervened.

'It is your id,' it said in a precise German accent. I felt a rush of gratitude. Doctor Bleeman, my psychiatrist, was here. He was going to help me through this... this relapse. My muscles felt taser-locked (don't ask how I know) and I ended up rotating my whole body left.

It wasn't Dr. Bleeman. It was a worse nightmare, a new one, and a very large one, squatting imperiously on matted black kangaroo haunches that segued into the scaly, sea-green torso and head of a seahorse. There were shoulders. Very wide, heavy shoulders with polished logs the color of unripe bananas for arms. An ideal NFL lineman if the head had had eyes. Layers of translucent yellow tendons joined arms to shoulders. The near log dimpled like a cardboard tube in a half-dozen places on the way down to a wormy cluster of little pink tentacles delicately gripping a fan of playing cards with the ACBL logo. The cluster on the end of the other limb enfolded a large bulb of pale pink liquid.

It was a lot to take in, which is why I was slow to notice a pint-sized creature that resembled an Assyrian gremlin straight out of an archaeological dig perched on the imposing chitinous mound of the shoulder nearest me. Chicken claws festooned with pink suckers on the bottoms anchored it. It regarded me with ancient eyes, red and feline, a basalt chunk of evil. Small pointed ears swiveled forward. Armless shoulders hunched. As I looked back blankly, the larger creature's pipestem snout, which was the size of my forearm, split open just enough to reveal multiple rows of serious triangular teeth, and the limb holding the bulb kinked inward at successive joints to reach up and squirt a hefty dollop of the contents into it. A child-size dollop went into the toothless smile-parody of its little companion (pet? kibitzer?). Then it squirted a viscous stream into my face, simultaneously unfolding the card-holding limb to reach over and push my nerveless hand into my nose. It was rather unmistakable what it wanted. I realized the first words I'd heard had nothing to do with psychology; it'd been telling me it was my bid. It couldn't get its... whatever... around a 'b'. Evil-smelling goop, like absinthe decanted from an overflowing ashtray, dripped from my chin.

'Hold your horses!' I barked in retaliation, surprising myself with my fluency in hillbilly — and my fearlessness; for some reason, I was no more intimidated than if I had been dealing with my bratty niece. I used my cardigan's sleeve to wipe my face, and the vapor irradiated my nostrils with the intensity of Kentucky moonshine. If the drink was an alcohol analog, I had a mean drunk on my hands.

'Why would one hold such a large animal? You aren't someone your kind considers a 'ervert, are you?' it hectored. I was astonished to see the deep voice coming from the shoulder troll, its little devil-ears now flattened backwards.

A symbiote. A living mouthpiece. Its narrow lipless mouth explained the absence of heavily aspirated consonants. (I did make some classes at university.)

'You must excuse him,' interrupted a soft contralto from my right. *Mom?* I did another Frankenstein pirouette, only to face the creature's identical twin.

'My male offshoot has the intolerance of his sex,' Mom's voice continued, louder once the source leaned out from its roost on the far shoulder and peeked under the snout of its... host. 'We are Oroni. You are now 'art of our collection.' I did the emotional equivalent of windmilling my arms for balance, thinking: *Me and a wooden farm gate.*

So flattered. I supposed I should have been grateful not to be asphyxiated and pinned to a board. 'This 'game' in your head (the mimicry was so faithful I could hear the quotation marks) is of interest to us. Our machine flowers have scanned you and have created the normal environment for it.' *Not without some serious wire-crossing, you haven't.* 'We understand why you don't get smaller when you contract to 'lay the hand, and the intricacy of the 'lay, according to your god, Kelsey, is fascinating, 'ut this "Swiss" is most intriguing. You must demonstrate it for us.' *So much for extraterrestrial babes wanting to know about 'this thing you call "love"'*, my unvoiced portion of the dialogue continued. I felt like a wiseass version of the man-apes gibbering in front of the black monolith.

'You have "teammates" in the direction 'erpendicular to your dorsal surface.' Meaning I should turn around. I swiveled all of me in the folding chair (carefully, since I didn't know if its carnivorous tendencies had been replicated) and looked. Half a tennis court away, behind a shimmering transparency that divided the room, was an identical linen-shrouded table with two more of the Schwarzenegger-deVito combos. There was no mistaking the barrier for a giant monitor, however, because seated on the left of a scaly sea-green back was Loki.

The slender curves of the horns that sprouted like giant question marks from his shining golden helmet towered over even his outsized companions. The art-deco head-fortress exposed just enough of his vulpine features to see his dark eyebrows waggle at me. In full ponce mode, he followed up with a dainty finger-waggle and a swishy crossing of his muscular legs, a chancy proposition in his suitably scaled-up but still authentically rickety folding chair. It milked a nostalgic smile out of me despite what his presence signified. Seeing him sheathed in his familiar emerald Spandex ('very goddy,' he'd punned) was less of a shock than having a hybrid Anubis pop up in front of me. Opposite him sat...

Holmes.

Oh my god. He looked exactly — sallow warrior-saint features, proto-smile — as I remembered in my thousands upon thousands of replays of that film loop of his last words. He should have been accompanied by *Phantom of the Opera* organ music and crashing thunder, but he was just sitting there, ramrod straight, prosaically holding his cards, the tails of his impeccable black morning suit dangling out the back of a folding chair. His tightly combed-back hair glowed black, its part a white razor slash. He looked over, and his grimly amused gray raptor eyes somehow gave me hope even as I quailed at his presence. Some teammates.

Oh, this was a good one. A real topper. Only a year's respite this time. Blasé certainly didn't describe my reaction, but the question of whether I was piled up in a field and unconscious or whether I was in the grip of alien abductors / the Supernatural / paranoid schizophrenia / Satan wasn't the burning issue it once would have been... although unconscious was still preferable to insane, I conceded. The other options slotted somewhere in between. I shrugged stiffened shoulders. *Just get on with it.*

I turned back around to my table. A phlegmy noise issued from an anonymous location. *Right. My 'id.* My artificially contracted muscles suddenly loosened again for whatever reason. Small mercy. For a paranoid moment my entire awareness centered on that region aliens are notorious for probing, but all was as it had been, and I hastily inspected my cards. I suspected I didn't want to find out what the consequences of balking at participation in this improbable but oh-so-concrete scenario would be. ('HO-O-O-GAN! COOLER!')

The hand was not immediately familiar. I had half-expected to recognize it, since everything else was supposedly culled from my attic. 'The cards are randomly generated,' said Junior. (Any other Oroni I would automatically have nicknamed Mac.) I hoped the timing was coincidental. If they didn't need a machine to read my mind, this was going to be one pointless exercise.

The hand, arranged:

♠ A Q
♡ A K 4
♢ A Q 9 7 3
♣ A Q 5

| 70 | Bridge Mix

Impressive, but ever the cynic, I had to ask myself how random would the hands have been if the game were rubber bridge.

I noticed a messily filled out convention card in front of me. My handwriting, my usual conventions. Basically the same as the Egyptian Standard I remembered, although I reminded myself Anubis and I would be on the same wavelength anyway if he *was* a fleshed-out memory. A pity that that would mean Holmes was too. I'd hoped that one day I'd somehow be able to confront him again, intimidating as the prospect was. Any price would have been worth paying for a chance to end the mystery of *his* genesis. I hadn't been in a coma with him, unlike my sabbatical with the pantheon of has-beens. I'd had plenty of time to question *them*, and a lot of good it had done me; they'd answered with a catechism of mythological hogwash I wasn't sure even they believed. But Holmes... well, it would be worth taking a shot with this putative doppelganger.

Still my 'id. I stammered out 'Two clubs.' Junior's mouthpiece overcalled two spades in a neutral tone. This was reflected in its ears reverting, I presumed, to their default position, straight up and down. Prompted, I took notice of the gray metal duplicate board in the center of the table: we were vulnerable; they could get away with murder. I unthinkingly bid two notrump when the bidding came back to me unchallenged. I then asked myself why, but it was too late to double. Anubis, with a resigned I'm-going-to-waste my-life-as-dummy-again undertone in his new voice, raised to three. I never thought I'd miss his old scratchy whine. A tentacle whipped the seven of spades onto the tablecloth and I saw Anubis's self-pity was justified: I'd caused us to miss the boat by not doubling:

♠ J 5 4 3
♡ 8 6 3
♢ 6 5 2
♣ 10 7 4

```
    N
W       E
    S
```

♠ A Q
♡ A K 4
♢ A Q 9 7 3
♣ A Q 5

West	North	East	South
Junior	Anubis	Mom	Me
			2♣
2♠	pass	pass	2NT
pass	3NT	all pass	

From the lead, they obviously couldn't read minds unaided. East contributed the eight and I won with my queen.

Before I could gather my wits, a storm-crackled snippet of audio replayed in my head. 'Give a diamond, get a heart back.'

The radio ad. Really? Apparently my subconscious was scraping up a Message from Beyond out of sheer habit. Plus I was supposed to believe the Supernatural was phoning this one in. I mean, what else was I going to do but duck a round of diamonds, and why wouldn't the opponents switch to their best suit? Nevertheless I couldn't help feeling a bit like a hand puppet with Fate's hand up my ass when I led the diamond three. It went eight, two, a pause, and then a purposeful jack. Back came the scripted — *oh, big deal* — ten of hearts. Junior flicked out the queen when I won with my king. A clue, if he wasn't unblocking. Did it matter? My best hope was for the king of diamonds to fall out of sub-space (getting with the evening's *Close Encounters* theme), but barring that, if Junior had king-third, I could throw him in with it after I removed his spade and — hopefully — heart exits. Normally I would have had no reason not to go this straightforward route, but there was that pause to consider. Maybe she'd just been passing gas, or maybe my admittedly fragile ethics had suffered in translation, but it seemed likely his mom had something to think about. If they appreciated Kelsey, they probably were far enough beyond the Dick and Jane level not to fumble over a play like overtaking with a useless doubleton jack to lead through declarer.

So, if she didn't have a doubleton king-jack, how to arrange for a diamond finesse? A club worked if the Bad Seed on my left had the king-jack: lead the queen at him once I stripped his spade and heart exits. Dummy's ten would keep him honest; he'd have to put me over there one way or another, or lead a diamond himself, if he had one.

Or I could cash a spade... and duck a heart to his stiff jack! The sort of sexy little play beloved of bridge columns. It too was contingent on him having both club honors, but it would look fantastic on my résumé. I was in love.

Oops. What would I do if he exited with the *jack* of clubs? The king, even. *Hmm.* Unrequited love. Stuck back in my hand. Hardly a disaster, since it would be my ninth trick — if diamonds split. That was a concern. My Bols Brilliancy wouldn't look half as clever if they didn't. Frustrating. Another case for a Fantasy Hand of the Year award. Maybe he wouldn't find it. Or maybe I could throw him right back in with his club... and maybe lose too many tricks. *Arrgh.*

I was herding myself toward a cliff. I'd done it enough to recognize the signs. Back to the first (giggle) *Plan Mine from Outer Space.* I was acclimating.

How would it fare if Junior's ten was a singleton? If Junior cashed his spade and exited with a club, fine. Three spades, two hearts, two clubs, and the diamond finesse added up to my favorite integer. If he didn't, if he led a club right back or stayed with spades, problems. With the king not falling, a diamond finesse would be only eight tricks ... but wouldn't East's hand be running into trouble about then? If Junior had elected to return, say, a low club (the jack merely delaying things), after the finesse we'd be down to:

```
            ♠ J 5
            ♡ 8
            ◇ 6
            ♣ 7

♠ K 10 8         N          ♠ —
♡ —         W       E       ♡ 9 7 5
◇ —              S          ◇ K 8
♣ K 6                       ♣ —

            ♠ —
            ♡ 4
            ◇ A 9 7
            ♣ A
```

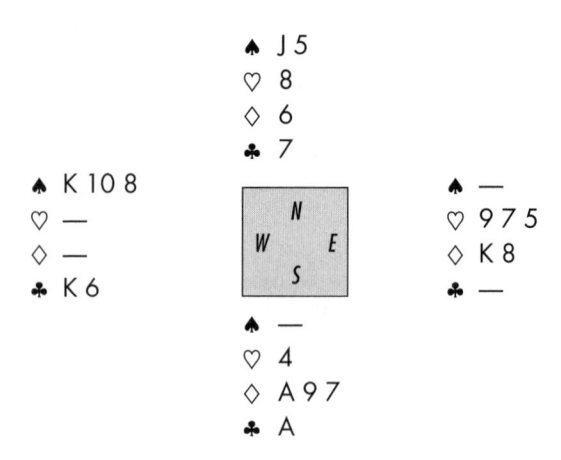

Sweet. The ace of clubs would squeeze a heart out of her; no more setting trick when I put her in with my brilliantly preserved four of hearts to cough up the last two tricks.

Junior fired out the heart jack when I cashed the ace. His mom showed out on my spade, letting go a club, upping the odds on an awkward diamond break. Now queen of clubs with bated breath...

No takers.

Hadn't thought of that. I guess it was pretty obvious to Junior what his fate would be. Not a bad play, ducking. It wasn't going to save him. *This'll look good on you, bozo.* Ace and out in clubs put him in to cash a fourth club and the king of spades — his mom bleeding red cards to beat the band — and then a flourish-free spade plopped on the table, putting me over in the promised land for my hard-won diamond finesse. Of course I didn't need it by then, since the jack of spades forced his mom to pare down to a singleton king of diamonds and a heart to cover the board's. Still, I preferred to treat it as a finesse on principle. You can never take enough winning finesses. They are God's way of telling you he loves you. And wishes to smite your enemies. Junior contributed two begrudging spades as the hand climaxed.

I was the *Man*! Well, in this freak show, more like *the* man, but still... Anubis gave me a toothsome grin and a mini-salaam. I almost felt bad about cherishing our time apart.

The full deal:

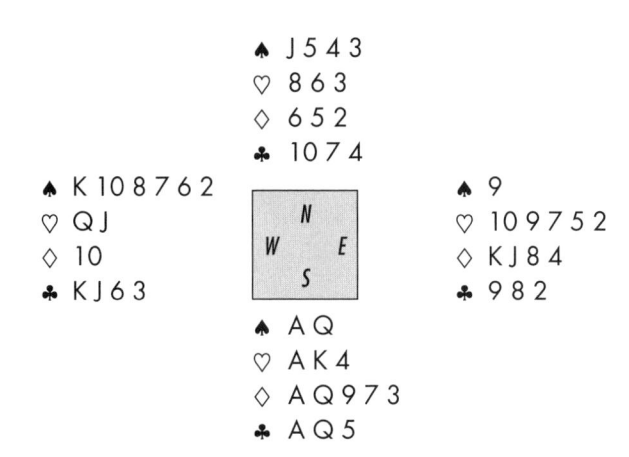

```
            ♠ J 5 4 3
            ♡ 8 6 3
            ◇ 6 5 2
            ♣ 10 7 4
♠ K 10 8 7 6 2              ♠ 9
♡ Q J          N            ♡ 10 9 7 5 2
◇ 10       W       E        ◇ K J 8 4
♣ K J 6 3      S            ♣ 9 8 2
            ♠ A Q
            ♡ A K 4
            ◇ A Q 9 7 3
            ♣ A Q 5
```

Junior tentacled the cards together and popped them in his mouth. Brown curlicues of vapor issued from a field of nostrils on top of his proboscis. The haunting tang of autumn fire tickled my nostrils. 'It is wasteful to incinerate food outside the body,' he/his mouthpiece/whatever chided us. Great. Yurassis Dragon channeling Al Gore. With a palate that would put a raccoon to shame.

Over the next seven boards the opponents exhibited an overall Flight B technical grasp, taking their obvious tricks and bidding routine games (both sides had two). A notable exception came in the trench warfare of partscores. There they proved to be LOLs. They seemed to think bidding was actually a science and assumed if we bid it, we must be prepared to make it, despite ongoing evidence to the contrary. We might be 'art of their collection, but we could bully them out of their lunch money. *Whoah. Did I just think 'we' about my mental illness across the table?* Anyhow, 'we' stood to be up a goodly amount of IMPs, depending: Loki's bidding could politely be described as mercurial. Ironic, considering Mercury had been a strict Roth-Stone adherent.

After the last board both Oroni again faithfully recorded the result in their ACBL (Alien Contract Bridge League?) scorecards — using green pens, no less — which were filled out with an exact duplicate of my barely legible scrawl. They lifted slightly, clutching the cards, and from the way they reversed away from the table I got the impression they weren't levitating all by themselves but were riding something. I

Close Encounters of the Unkind | 75 |

pictured them on broomsticks, sporting pointy black hats. A *Far Side* Halloween. It helped.

They floated around me and sailed in line astern through the high-tech room divider as if it wasn't there, breaking the sound barrier, as it were, since that appeared to be its sole function; I'd looked over my shoulder once and seen Loki throw his head back in one of his echoing godlike peals of laughter and it had been in pantomime.

Loki arose and, for once, walked normally, crossing to us in four giant steps, his satiny emerald cape just starting to billow as he got to us.

'You didn't say "May I",' I greeted him, having gratefully abandoned my bum-muncher to stand.

He gave me a pitying look. Fitting, someone so jaded would have jade eyes. Holmes, whose strides weren't short either, veered over to the 'corner' twenty feet to my right, where the smooth, faintly luminescent wall met the shimmering room divider, and turned his back to us. His right arm became a stump and his coat collar shifted as he retrieved something from inside the coat. Then he took the coat off and threw it on his left shoulder. He undid a silver cufflink on that arm, shoved it into his pants pocket, and rolled up his sleeve to reveal a rangy forearm. He had a syringe in his teeth. He made a fist, flexed the arm, and gave a spot below the elbow several hard taps with two fingers. The arm moved out of sight and the other retrieved the syringe. Several long seconds later his whole body gave an embarrassingly orgasmic shudder. The back of his head dipped low as he slumped and leaned his forehead against the wall.

Awwk-waard. Not a good time for question period. This old home week just kept getting better.

We circumspectly ignored him as he languorously reassembled his wardrobe. Loki remained standing, possibly because he didn't trust his weight on the table. The chairs would have been suppositories. I stood, getting mildly dizzy, and he held his scorecard at elbow height while I held mine up like an auction paddle so we could compare. Anubis came around and looked over my shoulder expectantly. Microwave a wino's undershorts and you'd approximate his breath.

'What'd you lead against three no on board one?' I asked Loki, like it was an ordinary day at a sectional in Daytona. He had plus fifty.

'A spade,' he replied in a mellifluous upper-class British accent. It echoed around his cavernous sinuses before coming out, but it was Holmes's voice. They hadn't quite got Loki right either. Or he was screwing with me, which wouldn't have been out of character. The real Holmes's eyes glittered, partially in amusement at his own apparent facility for ventriloquism. His face was flushed, i.e. pale ocher.

'They play a big club,' he continued, 'so I checked them out with two spades and they let me live, so I talked myself into leading one.' Anubis and I made brief eye contact — hard to be sure with him — but he didn't squeal on me. 'The goblin's ride turned as purple as Joe Biden at a press conference when dummy's spades came down.' He shook his head, the tips of his helmet's horns making airy doodles, and added, 'Couldn't tell if it was happy about the lead or unhappy I got away.' A potentially useful tell. The bizarreness of my first thought being 'potentially useful tell' was not lost on me. 'Then it ducked a diamond and the junkie overtook and pushed a club through. Even I couldn't have made it after that.'

'I got a heart return.'

'Hand sort of plays itself after that, doesn't it?'

'Er, yeah,' I replied, trying not to sound miffed at his cavalier dismissal of my otherworldly table presence. Of course I'd have done the same to him.

We went quickly through the rest of the list and it was what I'd expected. Except for his one fling, Loki had stayed within bounds and Holmes had, not unexpectedly, been letter perfect. We (I officially gave up trying to differentiate myself from them) were up 30 IMPs.

'Is winning such a good idea?' Anubis whispered conspiratorially. We looked at him. 'I'm just sayin',' he responded defensively. He had a point. The kid did have a temper. Nevertheless, it didn't seem like a good idea to roll over and let them think they'd mastered the game. I doubted I'd be put out to stud.

The alien confab broke up and half of them floated back toward us on their invisible skids. I assumed their mode of locomotion was a status thing or just plain laziness. Or had I been kidnapped by handicapped aliens? Or were their 'legs' reproductive organs? Who knew?

Close Encounters of the Unkind

When we all took up positions again, I couldn't tell if they had switched pairs. I hoped so; Junior was the type directors were on a first-name basis with, and not because they wanted to be.

LHO (Left Hand Oroni) used one 'hand' to unwrap a royal-blue linen packet that it had literally pulled out of thin air in front of it — a compartment in its conveyance. It began dealing, the dozen little tentacles on its arm working like oars on a war galley, rowing the cards out as the arm swung around the table. Oroni would never know the satisfaction of cracking their knuckles, but their icky digits were more supple than fingers and dealt the brittle cards as swiftly as any Vegas mechanic and more delicately. I was surprised when the cards didn't have any gelatinous residue on them. Did I mention that the card tray never got used? It was never rotated either, though the deal was, but it still governed vulnerability. I kind of wished they'd got their act together on that one; always being red was a real style-cramper.

It dealt:

♠ K Q 10
♡ A K Q 9 4
♢ A 2
♣ Q 6 5

It went the three expected passes to me, in querulous LOL voices from the Oroni, and I opted for two notrump. This time LHO passed. Anubis looked very put-upon, and Staymaned. An extra-querulous pass from RHO. I told him about my hearts and he raised to game. LHO let the ten of diamonds float from her (it seemed the right gender assignment) grasp. No flicking, which reminded me that Junior had better watch his mouthpiece. They might not have examined all the facets of Loki's personality when they borrowed him from me, and he was a *Viking* god.

Anubis's contribution made for a cold three notrump. Unfortunately, we were in four hearts.

```
              ♠ A 9
              ♥ 10 5 3 2
              ♦ K 6 4
              ♣ 10 7 4 3

                   N
                W     E
                   S

              ♠ K Q 10
              ♥ A K Q 9 4
              ♦ A 2
              ♣ Q 6 5
```

West	North	East	South
LHO	Anubis	RHO	Me
pass	pass	pass	2NT
pass	3♣	pass	3♥
pass	4♥	all pass	

It wasn't like he'd put us in a horrible spot. I could hardly question his judgment after what I'd perpetrated on the first hand previously, but you never like to see potential swings like this at IMPs.

I won in hand, cashed a heart, and sat back when RHO pitched a spade. Worst-case scenario. From no-brainer to brainer. Having someone to blame took the pressure off somewhat, but it would still be nice to make it. At that point, the next Message wannabe put in an appearance.

'You have to play clubs to keep it real,' it snapped and crackled in my head.

Oh, come on. That is so lame. But disturbing. I wished this crap would stop popping into my head; its applicability was becoming unsettling. I *was* going to have to play clubs. And I was going to have to be lucky. The good news was I didn't have to rely solely on finding outrageously fortuitous holdings; I could strip spades and diamonds and hope someone — specifically West, although Flight B East could easily be caught napping — had a doubleton ace or king of clubs, e.g.

Close Encounters of the Unkind

```
              ♠ —
              ♡ 10 5
              ♢ —
              ♣ 10 7 4 3
♠ 3                          ♠ 7
♡ J 8         N              ♡ —
♢ 7        W     E           ♢ Q
♣ K 2         S              ♣ A J 9 8
              ♠ —
              ♡ Q 9 4
              ♢ —
              ♣ Q 6 5
```

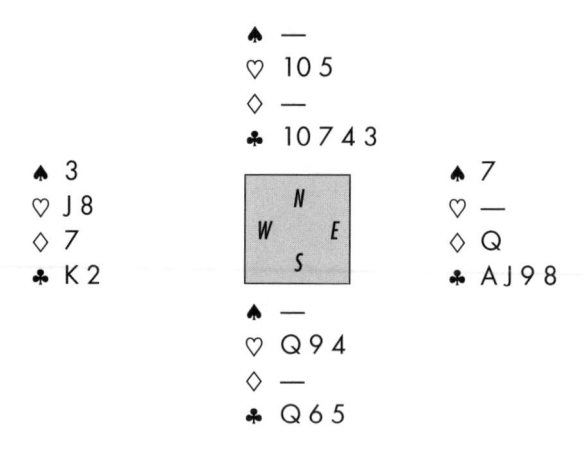

My queen was enough to prevent them taking more than two tricks in the suit before West got stuck on lead. She would have to give me a ruff-sluff unless she wanted to lead away from her trump holding. It wasn't Fantasy Hand of the Year material if it didn't work, but considering how the day's extracurricular activities were catching up to me, I, for one, was reasonably impressed, except I could already hear Loki laughing it off with 'Way to go, Garozzo! Refresh my memory — is this hand in every third syndicated bridge column out there, or just every second one?'

It turned out my luck was in. Sort of. I cashed spades to pitch a diamond from dummy and then cashed both diamonds, ending in dummy to lead a club. East played low, I played low, and West, after a pause during which her upper body rippled Biden purple (the first tell I'd seen and I was about to find out what it meant) won with the nine.

As you can see following, I'm still waiting for my ruff-sluff.

```
              ♠ A 9
              ♥ 10 5 3 2
              ◇ K 6 4
              ♣ 10 7 4 3
 ♠ J 8 4 3        ┌─────┐        ♠ 7 6 5 2
 ♥ J 8 7 6        │  N  │        ♥ —
 ◇ 10 9 8         │W   E│        ◇ Q J 7 5 3
 ♣ 9 8            │  S  │        ♣ A K J 2
                  └─────┘
              ♠ K Q 10
              ♥ A K Q 9 4
              ◇ A 2
              ♣ Q 6 5
```

I must admit the stupid 'Message' had lulled me; not that I would have done anything differently. Apparently my poor old battered subconscious couldn't shake the idea that the Supernatural had to be a pre-existing condition for these delightful Halloween treats, even if it was reduced to being no more than a harbinger of success. Now that it could demonstrably be relegated to mere random association, my heart didn't exactly take wing, but I did feel slightly less crappy about being taken to the cleaners by a Flight B talent. *Worth the price.* Any hybrid of the Supernatural and this... this freaking *cartoon* I was enmeshed in, was something I wasn't ready to deal with. I needed both hands to keep a grip on reason. I couldn't afford to use one waving a crucifix around.

Slightly-less-crappy was almost euphoria under the circumstances and a furtive rictus of a smile escaped, one I opportunistically expanded in hopes it would come across as self-deprecating, for Anubis's benefit. *Gosh, do I have egg on my face, or what?* Morale is important. I bet Alexander the Great had a great screw-up smile for his rare oopsies.

Naturally, it being such a *special* day and all, I had to suffer a sudden nasty setback: I remembered the idiot guitarist in the radio interview had also said, bitterly, 'But sometimes clubs will take you for a real ride, man.' Did it count if I was too brain-dead to resurrect what should have been the whole Message? A determined, only slightly shaky 'Bah, humbug!' was all I could come up with to quarantine any more troubling speculation. A bit like quarantining Hannibal Lecter.

Close Encounters of the Unkind | 81 |

On a positive note, I'd pinned down the purple tell. Winning a doubleton nine always made *me* happy.

It turned out that the first board had one indisputable harbinger — the result. The Oroni were ready to rock 'n' roll. Their defense continued unerring, their declarer play became pinpoint. The trenches turned into WWI. They stole a partscore from under our noses, then had the temerity to double us in an injudicious (read foolhardy) push on another one. The fact I was slow to catch on didn't help, and by the time I did I was too shell-shocked to do anything but play out the string. I'd had it too easy all day — bridge-wise — to shift gears that abruptly.

Our comparison after the mini-Armaggedon was predictably gloomy. It was at least recrimination-free; we'd all (well, perhaps not Holmes) been blindsided by the quantum leap in their ability. The four hearts I'd blown out my wee brainies in? Three notrump for them. We lost back our 30 IMPs. They were getting better. How much longer before we — I — became superfluous?

My personal gloom was shortly alleviated by the arrival of a floating picnic basket from a small iris that opened in the wall facing me. The basket wasn't covered and when it alighted on the table, I beheld a child's garden of earthly delights: Big Macs, fries, vanilla shakes, Pepsis, apple turnovers. The irreplaceable aroma of hot grease teased my sinuses. Unlike any time in my adventure among the pyramids, I discovered I was famished. At least I could eat this time around, I consoled myself as I slurped and crammed sugar and cholesterol into me. It could have been iced infant's blood and long pig and I would have done the same. I was the lone diner, not surprisingly; junkies don't eat and gods don't have to. At least, I'd never seen the Egyptians or any of the other defunct deities chowing down. Then again, I'd remained at one bridge table or another for the whole year. Maybe they'd feasted like crazy when I wasn't around — if they'd even existed when I wasn't around. I didn't even know what level of existence I'd been on.

It didn't take long to use up all my saliva, though I barely chewed before swallowing. Meanwhile, Holmes, seated beside me, whipped out his works, which consisted of a royal-blue Moroccan leather case that he flipped opened with a slightly shaking hand to reveal a trio of compact syringes belted in. The used one with its depressed plunger sat beside two fresh ones sparkling with a clear liquid, their silver plungers gleaming seductively. To him. Singularly off-putting to me. I knew how my great-grandfa... Watson must have felt. He then re-enacted his junkie liturgy before tidying himself up again and exchanging the case for a leather roll-up tobacco pouch the same color, together with a pipe and a colorful box of wooden matches from the limitless depths of his coat. The matchbox's label was a real collector's item, a white swan in a green square and, in white letters, 'SWAN' in an adjoining red square. Its legend trumpeted 'the smoker's match'. The pipe got clamped in his mouth and the pouch went on the table, where he proceeded to unroll it, pinch out a generous shag, and tamp that down in the bowl. The pipe was cherrywood and straight, not the bogus meerschaum popularized by Hollywood. In no time I was imprisoned in an aromatic cloud, as Loki and Anubis had borrowed matches and joined in, lighting up implausible Cohibas. Mutt and Jeff standing together in companionable silence, exhaling soulfully. The gods of present-day religions should be so ecumenical. The cloud dissipated, but not without a fight.

I had other issues as well. If I could feel hunger, then other bodily functions might not be far behind. Did the aliens have washrooms? Also, I could have used a roll of Tums. The Oroni, however, were nowhere to be seen. They might well have fled at the sight of me gorging myself.

Half a pipeful went by before I got up my courage, turned to Holmes with trepidation, opened my mouth to speak — only to have a large part of the back wall on the far side of the barrier iris open. The Oroni came stomping and roaring through like the New Zealand All Blacks. Okay, they didn't really do that — I couldn't have heard them anyway — but it sure seemed that way after the last set of boards. My determination faltered and Holmes rose effortlessly and followed Loki across the room, my unspoken questions swirling in their wake. *Catch you on the flip side*, I thought numbly, covering cowardice with cool.

I wasn't in the best frame of mind when we fixed bayonets and went at it again. I misplayed a partscore — no mini-salaam for that one — and followed that up by misdefending a game, fortunately only by an overtrick. It was extra upsetting because it was against Junior and his mom, and I had a hard-on for the hulking bastard. Either he hadn't overstepped the proprieties against Loki or Loki was mellowing. I was in my same chair, but Junior was now on my right, causing me to wonder if the Oroni were superstitious.

Merciless self-flagellation served to put me back on an even keel, albeit in choppy waters, and we parred the next three deals, which wasn't easy for either side. After we split back-to-back Montreal slams came this, the last hand:

♠ K Q J 9 8 6 4
♡ A 6 5
♢ Q
♣ A 9

By now my bladder was full and my stomach felt like it had gone native and was incinerating my food. I could also sweat, and I was doing so, profusely, despite the coolness. While I was wondering how to bid this one, Junior rendered it academic by opening three notrump. Does this always seem to happen to you, too? I leaned over to look at his scorecard, hoping, improbably, that a bloodbath was in the offing. No such luck. The range was blank and I managed to interpret 'my' scrawl underneath (I blame my chock-full-of-doctors family for my handwriting) as gambling, with an outside control.

'Major contracts can change your fortunes,' whispered in my brain, but I blurted out 'Four spades' before it finished. I didn't need prompting to make a bid that was staring me in the face; doing anything but overcalling on these auctions never seems to work out. But this third 'coincidence' didn't leave much room for doubt that the Supernatural was, if not directing this really, really off-Broadway production, then co-producing it — which didn't seem all that horrific at this point. No worse than having an intrusive kibitzer. Indeed, having its blessing was weirdly comforting, which showed how low my fortunes had sunk. Maybe someday, I speculated sardonically, it would be more useful, give me stock tips — though what I really needed was for the world to adopt a calendar that didn't have October.

I bought the contract, and a spasm of orange through Junior's upper body was easy to read. Not happy. First round, he would almost certainly have come back in with five diamonds, but they'd learned.

His mom let loose the diamond six and I waited, Depends-less, as Anubis methodically put his cards down.

Our assets:

♠ 5
♡ J 10 9 4 3 2
♢ 10 3
♣ K Q 6 2

```
    N
W       E
    S
```

♠ K Q J 9 8 6 4
♡ A 6 5
♢ Q
♣ A 9

West	North	East	South
Mom	Anubis	Junior	Me
		3NT	4♠
all pass			

Junior was going to be thoroughly pissed; he had nine tricks if he really did have an eight-card suit. He won his king of diamonds and tried the ace. I ruffed with the eight and his mom completed a high-low. An uppercut loomed if her beloved offshoot had the spade ace. I would need to lead from board to thwart it, which meant I'd have to risk three rounds of clubs right away for my heart pitch. Scary. On the bright side, his control might be in hearts, and I'd be fine as long as spades behaved. What to do, what to do...

Inspiration came, and best of all, it came solo. And lo, it was good. I chortled. Junior's vocal cords, having exchanged shoulders the better to glower at me, flattened its ears, and would have been hissing at me if it were a cat. In fairness, I do have an evil chortle.

I blithely led a high spade. He won and pumped another diamond out. I ruffed with the nine and his mom pitched a heart, not anywhere near instantly. I chortled some more when I led a high spade and Junior showed out. I managed to put a lid on the chortling as I drew

Close Encounters of the Unkind

trumps — I was even beginning to annoy myself — and conceded her ten. She dispensed the king of hearts.

This was the deal:

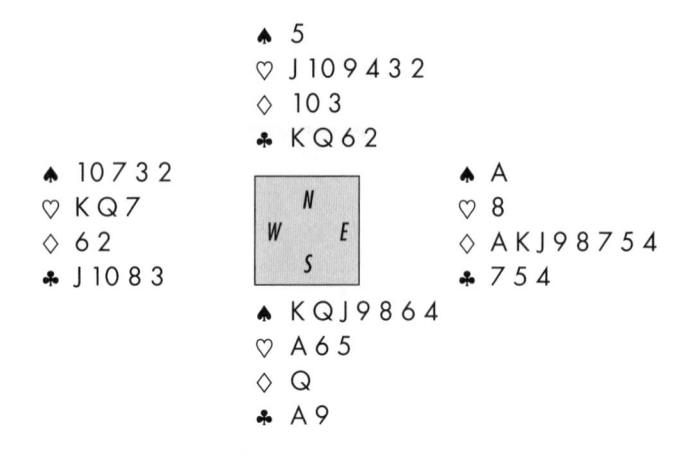

```
                    ♠ 5
                    ♡ J 10 9 4 3 2
                    ◇ 10 3
                    ♣ K Q 6 2
    ♠ 10 7 3 2                          ♠ A
    ♡ K Q 7          N                  ♡ 8
    ◇ 6 2         W     E               ◇ A K J 9 8 7 5 4
    ♣ J 10 8 3       S                  ♣ 7 5 4
                    ♠ K Q J 9 8 6 4
                    ♡ A 6 5
                    ◇ Q
                    ♣ A 9
```

And this would have been the ending if Junior hadn't spoiled my slow, tortuous dragging-out of each card (you've got to take time to enjoy the little things) by eating his cards as soon as he saw I had no more trump losers:

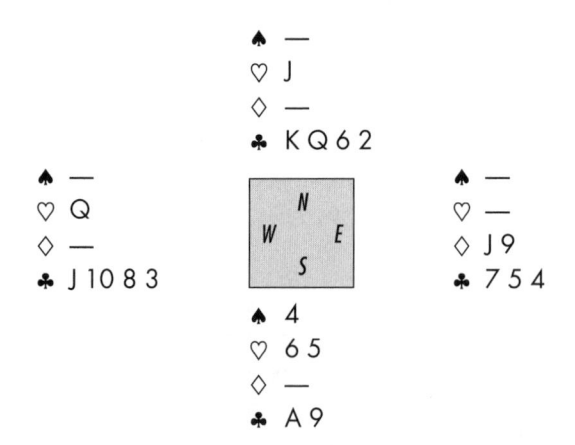

```
                    ♠ —
                    ♡ J
                    ◇ —
                    ♣ K Q 6 2
    ♠ —                                 ♠ —
    ♡ Q              N                  ♡ —
    ◇ —           W     E               ◇ J 9
    ♣ J 10 8 3       S                  ♣ 7 5 4
                    ♠ 4
                    ♡ 6 5
                    ◇ —
                    ♣ A 9
```

I was pretty proud of myself for seeing that my uppercut worry had been a phantom. The ace of spades being with East meant the king of hearts, and *almost* certainly the queen, would be with West, and if

| 86 | *Bridge Mix*

West could get an uppercut, voila — a rectified count. I could claim, since East wasn't going to be the one guarding clubs either. Of course, all this wondrous insight assumed a 3-2 spade break; with the 4-1 break, I was doomed if Junior had simply run a heart through me when he was back in. But that made my bridge confection extra sweet: now I had something to throw in *his* face... faces. Just because the uppercut might have been necessary if West had had fourth-nine of spades and the ace of hearts rather than the king-queen wouldn't make the outcome any less galling (or whatever organ they blamed for that sort of thing). The cherry on top was that he could see he'd kept us out of a hopeless four hearts.

Don't goad the grumpy alien, I cautioned myself, as everything above Junior's haunches, mouthpiece excluded, had become a Florida sunset.

Oroni not being much for small talk, they levitated away from the table and streamed toward the back wall, which obligingly spiraled open. The mouthpieces squawked at each other animatedly.

Despite my satisfaction, it was a tense few minutes for us humans, er, non-aliens while we waited for the last board to be played at the other table. Anubis cracked his knuckles and doodled hieroglyphic-looking things in his card. I thought of ocean tides, rain, babbling brooks. *Aargh.*

When the other Oroni rotated away from their table and headed out their end of the room, I got up and trudged after Anubis. His walk was more of a slow-motion lope. Loki was smiling from ear to ear when we got there. With him, that could signify an ass-kicking either way. Holmes looked remarkably together — coolly deranged, if that's possible — considering he had to be high as a kite. We plunked ourselves down, a move I regretted when my bladder got compressed. It ceased to be a concern when Loki appropriated my scorecard and began comparing. I left it to him because his portfolio could well have included being god of arithmetic, and speed was all I wanted. I got the feeling, probably because 'we' had nothing more to teach them, that this had been the last set, and I didn't want to finish up with the Samsonite luggage and a 'thanks for playing' before I was put on exhibit in an alien diorama. Crushing their skulls was an opiate I dearly wanted to have to ease that transition.

Tension mounted as Loki tabulated out loud: 'Lose five. Lose two. Lose three. Push. Push. Push. Push.' Down 10 IMPs. Nobody spoke. It came down to my last deal.

'Win 12!' Loki shouted. Blood, I'm embarrassed to say, rushed to my groin, the same way it did for Dubya when he won the Republican nomination (footage you didn't see on the nightly news). I became understandably light-headed. Everything began ballooning in and out like a hokey 3-D movie.

'Wha' hoppen? They in four spades?' I gargled.

'Doubled, to boot,' Loki answered, lowering his voice from air raid siren to merely loud. 'Your friend' how strange that sounded — 'opened four diamonds and then had the —' a grin at Holmes, 'fine judgment to whack them out.' He pre-empted my next question. 'What would you have done,' he asked, 'if your opponent won the diamond lead and returned a club?' There was admiration in his voice. The object of it had sparkly eyes and giggled.

'A club?' I asked stupidly. 'Why I'd probably—'

It hit me.

'Diabolical, isn't it?' Loki said. 'It out-Grosvenors Grosvenor. You can play clubs, take your pitch, and make your spade holding impregnable with a lead from board. But East obviously wants a club ruff, so you *can't* cash them now, *can't* lead a spade from board. Imagine your relief when West doesn't pop on your next spade. Imagine your astonishment after East wins — and leads another club. No accidental squeeze has developed' — I bristled half-heartedly — 'and declarer gets to fall on his sword when the bad trump break he could have nullified is revealed. Sheer perverse genius!' Loki grinned. 'I saw the *Jormungandr* at your table,' he said. 'You think *it* went psychedelic? Should have seen ours.'

I looked at Holmes surreptitiously, something niggling. If he was a construct, a graft from me, as I had been told, how on earth — poor choice of words — did he come up with a defense that would never have occurred to *me* in a million years? Did that mean...?

The wall at our end of the room irised open and only one Oroni glided out on its magic carpet. I too felt like I was floating. In urine.

It came to a halt, and its demonic epaulette glowered and leaned forward, ears pricked.

'Your 'roclivity to transcend logic is disharmonious for us,' he — for it was Junior — announced. It figured. He was a natural hatchet man. 'We cannot tolerate this.' A race of sore losers. That couldn't be good 'We do not wish —' a monumental effort '— to be your bitches.' His public address system's mouth relaxed again. 'You will be returned.'

I turned to Holmes, my mouth opening to speak, to question…

A bright light I was going toward turned into a flashlight jiggling toward me, its glow screened by flickering stalks of corn. I lifted myself on my elbows and the first sensation I had was a burning need to floss my scum-covered teeth. My mouth burned from apple-flavored lava. The second was that my bladder was no longer being the Mongol horde of organs. I hoped a wetness in my crotch was condensation from the lumpy mat of crushed cobs I was lying on. It — the corn — smelled like moldy bread. Thin gauze veiled the moon (*the* moon, good old Luna), which was bathing the clearing in pastel grays. I went to sit up, regretted my carelessness instantly, hissed in pain, and ever so gently levered my stiffened corpse over onto one elbow, working in stages. I could see the Infiniti upside down in the dimness, balanced on its roof, but not discernibly the worse for wear. It was fifty feet away on the other side of the flattened circle of harvest-ready corn I was in. Upright stalks formed a dark ring-wall, no breaks anywhere. I was in a crop circle.

The last stalks in front of me were pushed aside and a burly state trooper clad in a well-upholstered winter uniform coat stepped through. His light blinded me. All I could make out was the silhouette of his Smokey hat against the heavens. Seeing I was harmless and not dying, he played the flashlight around the curved perimeter, stopped for a long moment at the overturned car, then rotated it more methodically, twisting his body along with it, looking for the car-sized gap that had to be there. When he couldn't see one, the light came back to me.

'What's this, then?' he asked in an improbable Irish brogue.

'Trick or treat,' I replied, giving him my best jack-o'-lantern smile. Then I threw up on his boots.

Aliens

In space, no one can hear you bid.

Well, at any rate, very few listen. The good thing is, be they human or alien, head, no head, solid or squishy, they don't listen to each other either. The same as back on Earth. Pigeons are pigeons everywhere. My great-great uncle, when he was teaching me the game, used to constantly reiterate that I'd never lack for pigeons. I was four at the time, and I wasn't sure how those goofy birds in the park could even hold onto cards, but the old boy had a way of making pronouncements I couldn't forget. I'm a walking treasure trove of the arcane, thanks to him. I was glad he'd been around when I was a kid. Kids always prefer black sheep. More interesting. Somebody had to prick the pomposity balloon (so it seemed to me) that my workaholic doctor family floated around in. Puzzlingly, I was named after him, our middle names — John Hamish — honoring some ancestor or other who had started the family industry back in the twentieth century. The rejuve treatments had kept Gray (from Gray Gray Tunkel, the sobriquet I had bestowed on him when I was learning to talk) around well into his one-fifties. He only played social bridge by then with what he called his coterie of homey pigeons.

I remembered being dragooned (an example of aforesaid arcania) into Halloween candy distribution duty the last few years he was alive. Not an inappropriate job, since I was built like a Pez dispenser. (Look it up.) I was barely older than some of the kids who came to the door. It wasn't the best way to spend my birthday evenings, but he always made it up to me. He'd sit on the couch, comically nervous and slugging back scotch. He never talked about what instigated this aberrant — even for him — behavior. Apparently it wasn't childhood trauma; I was told Halloween hadn't been anything but an excuse to party, up until he was in his twenties. Intriguing.

Now here I was, probably a carbon copy (hint: has nothing to do with cloning) of his own youthful self. I made my living hustling on these inter-system liners. Who'd have guessed the one outstanding thing humanity would bring to the galactic table would be cards? Good old time-wasting shuffle-and-deal cards. Games are universal to the hundreds of sentient species comprising the Conglomerate — analogs of chess were common up until each species' computer age rendered them academic — but bridge had struck like a virus among the Oroni after their clandestine and highly unethical field trips to Earth, and then it had infiltrated everywhere. Regardless of the official altruism line taught in school, the possibility of variations on this addiction was what had really driven the Conglomerate to waive the usual requirement for development of faster-than-light travel and welcome Earth with open arms — and whatevers — as soon as we had self-sustaining colonies on Mars.

Now poker is also hot with the younger civilizations. By younger, I mean ones that aren't heard-the-Big-Bang ancient: societies anything from tens of millennia to a few million years old. Of the Founders, the aristocratically feline Brog find endless giggles from ingesting their brand of liquid intoxicant (the other commonality besides oxygen-breathing) and playing 'Go Fish', an indication of why their Empire would have driven Genghis Khan to apoplexy. It has, however, lasted fifty million years.

I had a few days till the next planetfall and I hadn't been doing too well at the table. The card gods seemed intent on building my character, and if the three amazing women who'd divorced me couldn't do that, what was the point? I'd eked out enough to eat as long as I could stomach the recycled food the wait staff got fed (every bit as tasty as it sounds; no use wasting the real thing on the *hoi polloi*) and maybe enough to pay for passage on my next ship, but nothing for the extended R&R in between I so coveted.

I wandered hopefully into the plushly cavernous and sparsely populated lounge and stood for a moment inside the side entrance's panoramic arch, hypnotized by the enormous elliptical eye of the viewing portal across the way. Mountainous as it was, it was a fraction of what constituted almost the entire side of the unthinkably large ship. It was like an iridescent compendium of alien sunsets, supra-light stars smearing by in every color the eye or any sight organ could register. There were plenty of other spectacular venues for socializing on the ship: a deck of hanging gardens a hundred times larger and more exotic than Babylon's, and a beach/waterfall that was Waikiki meets Niagara, to name a couple — but this one never got old for me. There were worse fates than to be the Flying Dutchman, sailing those coruscating seas for all eternity.

I reluctantly tore my eyes away and looked around. The place served as a departure lounge, and when all the below-deck furniture was elevated in a few days, it would be as crowded as a park on the first warm day of spring. For the moment, enclaves of video stations with everyday tables and chairs and couches were scattered across the vast cinnamon-colored carpet like way stations on a prairie. But, as expected, there was a foursome going at it nearby.

One of the foursome was a human male, a bit of a shocker; I'm a rarity this far from the Rim. Their table was close to the soaring multi-level bar that stretched like the superstructure of a mammoth sea-going luxury liner along my side of the lounge. With each deck kaleidoscopically checkered with the myriad shades of color preferred by whatever denizens were partying in any given segment, it was a wonder in its own right, an ordered, static fraternal twin to the viewing portal's wild surging. A cathedral to intoxication. A pub crawl would have taken me well into old age.

Stalking his prey, the pot-bellied lounge lizard steals into ambush. I pushed back my sleeve and pretended to look at my chrono as if I was waiting for someone and strolled over to a cluster of quasi-club form-chairs at a circumspect distance from the quartet. I touched one and it morphed, scaling down to accommodate me. As if being abruptly exposed to vastly superior technology wasn't enough to create a racial inferiority complex, why do we also have to be lawn jockeys in the size spectrum? I plopped into its overly intimate cupping of my buttocks and picked up a discarded newspaper off the table to kill time until I could cut in, keeping one eye on my future companions.

It's silly of us to call a computer membrane a 'newspaper', but we still cling, don't we? A knee-jerk reaction to being inundated by change. I was of the second generation that had grown up since First Contact, but the overwhelming culture shock still reverberates. It made what had suddenly become anachronisms precious to us, something to keep the flame of our identity burning. It doesn't explain lawn jockeys. I have our miraculously intact family Bible stored away along with a hoard of antique bridge books (not Gray's; he'd apparently destroyed his years ago), but most people's only contact with paper these days came from the rolls next to a toilet. I never travel anywhere without a trunkful myself; even a peripatetic adventurer like me hasn't adapted to picking chiggers out of a holding tank and letting them have a go at my nether regions as per the practice most everybody else has adopted from the Brog. The galaxy can be a vast and disgusting place.

The sheet read my vitals and displayed mainly Terran-related articles in Standard. I'm being politically correct in not calling it English. I'm glad Chinese didn't win out; talking through my adenoids gives me a headache.

It had been so long since I'd seen a fellow human that it was hard not to stare. Part of the reason was his looks and his wardrobe. Tall and aristocratic, with an ebony widow's peak capping sallow ascetic features, he was decked out in a gorgeous archaic outfit I recollected was called a morning suit, possibly because it took all morning to get into. From what I'd read, it was hallmark of the Doolittles, the Victorian Revivalists whose style was all the rage among our leisure classes. Black tails, silvery vest, silver watch fob, and an immaculate white shirt surmounted by a high, stiff collar and a tightly cinched narrow black bow tie completed the ensemble. A straight-stemmed pipe and an ashtray were close at hand. I can't understand the resurgence of a practice as disgusting as smoking. Who'd have thought a cure for cancer would have a downside?

As I skimmed impatiently, my stomach snapping at its tail, I happened upon my horoscope and wondered, as I often did, why those had survived now that so many constellations could be viewed from inside out or from any distorting angle (Cassiopeia, the anorexic frog). Anachronism Squared. It told me in its roundabout touch-as-many-bases-as-it-could prose to listen to what the little voice in my head told me. Good thing I wasn't a nascent serial killer, I noted judiciously.

I had barely finished the comics above it when one of the players, a Brendinian, a hulking lizard in a comical pink gauze tunic, rose on his tripod of tail and haunches, and stalked off in a huff. Nobody huffs like a Brendinian. The spectacle of what looked like a giant transvestite lizard — only males appear in public — stomping off like he was heading for Tokyo (classics never die), his sagittal crest a crimson flame, thick legs pumping, massive triangular tail in full harrumphing mode as it switched like a bucking firehose, would put a smile on your face if you were in front of a firing squad. I sprang to my feet, aided by the four-fifths Earth gravity, and semi-bounded over before the game could break up.

'What ho, gentleman,' I hailed them in Galactic as I reached back and dragged a formchair away from a video terminal. At least that's what I think I said; some of the clicks and esophageal growls were tricky. I have to be careful when introducing myself because my name is only a few glottal stops from being an admission of having a desire for sex with your parents. That was only polite for a couple of species. 'May I join you?'

Confronted by my proletarian assault, the man, on my right took no offense, merely raked me with arctic-gray predator eyes, curious. It gave me a chill. I was standing close enough to see the smooth silver-gray spats over gleaming black shoes that crystallized his perfection, which in turn caused my own whimsically recycled outfit, a somewhat worse for wear zoot suit — purple at that — to wilt around me. In my defense, I obviously wasn't expecting to get laid. I pulled down the brim of my formerly rakish big-brimmed fedora to hide as much of me as possible and introduced myself to the table. After the others acknowledged me, he did me the courtesy of using Standard. 'Mickey Spillane,' he said in a mellifluous light baritone with what I recognized from old movies as the upper class English accent favored by his ilk. Why does it automatically cow people? I suspect it even works on those who don't speak the language. How else to explain the way the English had, by their own admission, 'muddled through' the building of their empire.

'Why does that sound familiar?' I asked.

'A famous literary figure from the nineteenth century,' he replied with a thin, enigmatic smile that nevertheless thawed his eyes. I didn't feel quite so much like a meal. *Definitely a non-pigeon vibe there, though*, I thought uneasily. *Maybe I should wait for another game.* However, my grumpy stomach reached back and bitch-slapped my spine until it stiffened.

Across from him, webbed loosely into its self-spun sling suspended from a tall hook anchored to the deck for just that purpose, a chitinous orange Alice-in-Wonderland caterpillar — a Caroller — politely fixed me with all six eye-stalks. They were totally incongruous in his otherwise vulpine face. A proto-male by his color, and a high mucky-muck by the black diaper thingy on his slick, bifurcated bottom third — his legs — and the number of braids in the filaments crowning his outsize head. He introduced himself as #≅p7 (rhymes with *p7). Real tongue calisthenics. His three sets of supple tubular upper arms rippled up and down the sides of his narrow thorax in greeting. A tad unnerving. It was like the creepy *wahine* beckoning of a carnivorous plant. I was glad the heavy-duty lower ones didn't join in. He professed to be honored to meet another of the inventors of this marvelous game. His mild red flush corroborated that, according to the AI crystal fixed geosynchronously above the table. Its weirdly nasal Galactic — a compromise that didn't grate exceedingly on anybody's auditory receptors but didn't sound pleasant to anyone — interpreted the color change as a blend of self-abasement and gratitude analogs. (Needless to say, the crystal didn't do this while a game was in progress.) That wasn't something you could take to the bank, though I couldn't see how buttering me up would be worth the effort. Color changes supplied the emotional subtext of their speech, but by the time they reached the imago stage, like this one — in a sort of reverse butterfly maturation — they were fully capable of making the equivalent of goo-goo eyes at you while poisoning your drink. In other words, they're kissing cousins, only crunchier. They are homebodies who don't often travel outside their troika of star systems, so most people haven't heard of them, but I have a cousin who'd been on our first delegation to their home planet.

Funny story — they acquired their nickname when the delegation was directed to the wrong coordinates ('snafu' translates readily) and disembarked amidst what it supposed at first was a massed chorus of joyous greeting from hundred of locals. Turned out it was the frenzied ululations of a mating cluster in full *flagrante delicto*. Talk about egg on your face — literally, for those who got too close.

Across from me was a pale green creature I'd seen in pictures, but never encountered. A Heeby-Jeeby. The *raison d'être* for the name wasn't obvious, for unlike many of the other ambulatory nightmares we've acclimated to, he was humanoid, a bulky smooth-skinned mesomorph's mesomorph, only with a lot more joints than usual. I figured he could probably bend his limbs like pipe cleaners. (A product which, I confess, I am indebted to pipe smokers for; I do a sort of chain-link origami with them for therapy. It beats knitting, and real origami requires talent.)

The portals to whatever soul he had regarded me unreadably, unblinkingly. They were large black iris-less craters set in a broad moon face — literally; it resembled old cartoons of the Man in the Moon, pockmarked green cheese part included. The Fu Manchu moustache was a discrepancy, true, and when I looked more closely and saw it was actually thin wormy tendrils undulating disconcertingly around his lipless mouth, his name seemed less of a mystery. I assumed he *was* a he; unless he was a nudist, his was one of the species that didn't much care for clothes — like the Rigellans, who still elicited an occasional sophomoric giggle from me — and from my vantage point I had a clear view of a webbed foot casually crossed over a weight-lifter's thigh framing a... male protrusion. In his case, it was a set of wicked-looking pincers resembling a nastier version of a shark's claspers. Less kinky than some, though. Remember the Brendinian's sagittal crest? It was for display, yes, but guess what it displayed. (Again, boys and girls, the galaxy can be...?)

'My designation is Shoolah,' his compressed lips hissed in otherwise accentless Standard.

I gaped at him, nonplussed. Spillane's head snapped around; apparently this was new to him too. It was very impressive. Terrans are a one-trick pony (some kind of small quadruped you sat on) as far as other civilizations are concerned — not unjustly — and our entry in any encyclopedia usually consists of a footnote under 'Bridge' and other card games. To have someone from a race I'd barely heard of bother to get a neuroprint of our backwater language made me feel simultaneously like a teacher's pet and a churlish clod for my complete ignorance of his. I was flustered enough that I executed something appallingly close to a curtsy.

'Shall we begin?' followed in businesslike Galactic as he surveyed the table. A creature after my own heart, I thought warmly, straightening self-consciously: no mention of stakes. I could taste the real meat and the margaritas at my eight-star hotel, perhaps in New Rio this time. Stomach was already booking passage and issuing dire warnings about any cancellation. I sat.

Me being the newbie, the deal fell to me. I shuffled awkwardly — might as well stay in character. I took time to enjoy the sensual slide of the omni-textured smart cards across my fingertips as I distributed them around the orange baize. I also took time to savor the exotic pot-pouri of alien skin excretions — sweet, mordant, the whole gamut — and the lingering ordure of expelled gasses. Added some of my own. The alien concoction, no matter how varied its composition, was always a stimulant. It always brought home the knowledge that I was undoubtedly going where no man had gone before. I also had the occasional dizzy spell from the ship's Tibetan atmospheric pressure to remind me I wasn't in Kansas anymore. I'm too lazy to exercise my way to adapting to it, so I take oxygen pills. #≅p7 would have been doing the same with hydrogen sulfide pills to supply the slightly higher concentration that most of the rest of us found disagreeable. Everybody's atmospheres are an amazingly compatible smorgasborg, but Rigellans have a lock on multi-species passenger shipping because theirs is the happiest medium.

I picked up, but as Gray had taught me, didn't sort:

> ♠ K 2
> ♡ Q 7 6
> ♢ K 6 5 2
> ♣ A Q 3 2

A pleasant way to start — a harbinger, I hoped — even if the Rigellan face cards were rather disturbing hieroglyphs of ancient rulers doing things Vlad the Impaler would have balked at. I bid one club, and Stinky, having reverted to his default orange setting, burbled one diamond. A hissed negative double from partner, a studious pass from RHO. Nice to have a human in the game, even if his blade of a face didn't rate to be a directory of tells. I bid one notrump, Stinky passed quickly, and partner took the money shot.

While Stinky was in the tank, partner proffered his cards and gestured with his other three-fingered claw that I should do the same. I complied warily and readied the needler in my sleeve-case in the event he reacted badly. You never know, and it can be the Wild West out here. He fanned the unsorted cards and the skin ringing his eyes irised halfway across them, answering my question about how they regulated light intake. His reaction could have meant anything from approval to blinding rage. We exchanged again, and Stinky finally finished communing with himself and produced the ten of hearts. I saw our combined assets for the first time (I had been too busy keeping an eye on him to inspect his half):

♠ Q J 9 5
♡ A K J 5
♢ 7 4
♣ 10 5 4

```
    N
W       E
    S
```

♠ K 2
♡ Q 7 6
♢ K 6 5 2
♣ A Q 3 2

West	North	East	South
#≡p7	Shoolah	Spillane	Me
			1♣
1♢	dbl	pass	1NT
pass	3NT	all pass	

I was happy to escape a diamond lead, even if an eighth trick would not have been unwelcome. I surveyed my domain grimly before playing dummy's ace. Always keep 'em guessing. Any chance to help an opponent fritter away his brain — or brains. East played an in-tempo four. I encouraged with my seven.

Another round, if you please.

There was a voice in my head.

Now, my subconscious is wont to keep secrets from me (part of its job description) and I'm used to it throwing out autocratic dictums, but they are always sensed first — that flash called inspiration — before getting spewed out where my conscious mind acts as midwife, spanking them to life, cutting the dark cord that wants to reel them back to oblivion, then wrapping them in words and decipherable images. That's how it's done with everybody, I assume. But this one came without the *Eureka!* burst, and it boomed like God delivering the Ten Commandments — politely — without any of the usual jagged, jumbled visuals to accompany it. It just rode in overtop of my conscious mind's machination's like they were a hyper-fast movie by a crazed *auteur* and it was a slow, deliberate voice-over. Granted, it had to override Stomach's nattering, but why was it using Spillane's voice? It seemed England had planted one more flag.

This was all pretty spooky. Hard to laugh off, but I'd dealt with worse; my younger days had been a haze of the newly minted psychotropic drugs that all the advances in chemistry had bestowed. I knew how to compartmentalize weirdness, and I did. Time for introspection later. I had a more pressing problem.

Off-putting though the freakishness of presentation was, I couldn't see any harm in complying. No reason it *couldn't* be from God, right? I shrugged. I played a heart to my queen. All followed, East with the eight. When I next led the spade king, Stinky didn't win it. Couldn't. He showed out, pitching the ten of diamonds. East ducked casually.

Not good news. Only two spade tricks, and those at the cost of East pounding diamonds through me. And no hope clubs would supply a lot of tricks; even without Stinky's overcall — pretty skimpy I might add — it would have been obvious East couldn't have a whole lot if he didn't think his seven-card suit was worth mentioning. Still, I didn't know what else to do, so I led another spade, steaming full speed ahead into the reefs. Maybe Stinky had his own seven-card suit and Spillane had no diamonds. Maybe that was why he hadn't pounced on the first spade. Stinky tossed a heart this time, and East won dummy's queen and plunked down the jack of diamonds.

I wasn't frozen in fear. I had begun to see the light. The queen would have been the best diamond to see, but any card Stinky found duckable was a great one if he did have the six-card suit one would expect to excuse his otherwise execrable overcall. If he didn't, I would have to drop back and punt. Gray used to say that. I really must look it up sometime.

I false-carded with my six — fritter, fritter — and awaited developments. Stinky pondered a long time before playing small.

East impassively shifted to a low club.

Gosh, that was swell. I happily played low and Stinky won his... king! *Huzzah!* He had evidently been around us humans a lot more than I would have guessed, because he shrugged before leading one back, and that was the end of the deal:

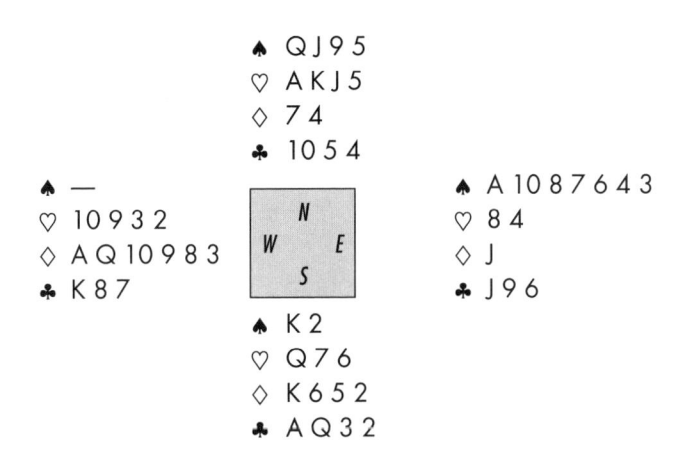

```
                ♠ Q J 9 5
                ♡ A K J 5
                ♢ 7 4
                ♣ 10 5 4
♠ —                                   ♠ A 10 8 7 6 4 3
♡ 10 9 3 2        N                   ♡ 8 4
♢ A Q 10 9 8 3  W   E                 ♢ J
♣ K 8 7           S                   ♣ J 9 6
                ♠ K 2
                ♡ Q 7 6
                ♢ K 6 5 2
                ♣ A Q 3 2
```

Such a simple play, that extra round of hearts. And so nice that East had that high diamond to allow West to leave him on lead. Note how hairy things get if he is left with a heart to exit. As you can see, I can then endplay Stinky easily enough — but that's only for an eighth trick. As you can also see, he could safely have overtaken the jack and forced out my king, because that ruins the selfsame strip squeeze by removing *both* the board's diamonds; I no longer have one to throw him in with when I'm finished running the board's majors. *I* have to break clubs, so all he has to do is hang onto his king and wait to cash out. But I'd been counting on the fact that poor Stinky couldn't be certain I didn't have the ten of spades; after all, his partner had stayed mum at the one-level. Giving me my ninth trick when he was about to roll up the rest of his diamonds would be pretty humiliating. A high Caroller official can't afford to look that foolish. He might have to terminate himself. Bad for everyone. (They explode.)

As I sat back, Stinky, color unchanged, reached out and scooped up our cards. His non-chromatic body language was always a mystery, but the cards did seem to be getting heavily compacted. East merely smiled slightly to himself. The AI, acting as both director and recorder, announced the result.

I was a bit weirded-out, but relieved to have a cushion, and though I seldom indulge at work, I flagged down a passing waiter, a lumbering Rigellan with an empty tray the size of a tabletop tucked under his massive arm. He — there was serious dangling going on under his transparent apron — lurched to a stop like a cartoon hippopotamus who'd dropped his wallet. He listened with the universal half-closed eyes and slouch of bored waiters as I ordered a scotch. It's synthetic, but more than passable as a nerve tonic. Gray might well have differed. Unfortunately, protocol demanded I also offer for the others. I prayed they wouldn't take me up on it and force me to subsist on the carpet in my room if I didn't win much. It looked safe, since they all had full containers of liquid in front of them, but Stinky quickly tilted one of his Shiva arms and tossed back his tumbler of lumpy purple liquid, smacking his jagged jack-o-lantern lips in a very human manner before thanking me and saying he would greatly appreciate more of the same to the waiter. What had I expected from a giant parasite?

As the waiter turned away, I made a horrible connection. I looked at the orange fluff between his legs, looked at the orange baize. *Omigod.* Did I mention the Rigellans are the galaxy's most fanatical recyclers? Even of their dead.

Stinky's six sets of long spatulate fingery digits flashed cards across the — *brrr* — orange baize, momentarily distracting me with his dexterity. Thank god for the AI; I could never have told if he was rigging the cards and I'm a damned good mechanic myself.

I feathered through the somewhat unwieldy pile and the smart cards duly contracted until I could comfortably pick them up. I was glad the Brendinian wasn't in the game; the cards would have started out so large an errant one might have decapitated me. Present company, relative shrimps, were merely mutant basketball players. I fanned:

♠ J 4 3 2
♡ A 9 6
♢ A 9 8
♣ A 5 4

About time the card gods did some extended sucking up. Unhappily, after Stinky passed, so did partner. East, who was probably Lord of Someplace-That-Had-Ceased-To-Exist, bid one heart in his Westminster voice. Very strange, hearing the voice in my head coming out another speaker. I doubled, Stinky burbled a slow two clubs, and partner made a sibilant responsive double. East passed without any problem and I bid my scraggly spades. This made me declarer.

Stinky flicked the eight of hearts on the table, perhaps to forestall any exchange, but Shoolah was not to be denied. It seemed he could take a hint, however; he gave my cards a quick once-over and handed them back while they were changing size. This didn't give me time to look at his before he nabbed them back with his other claw. He swiftly arrayed them and I saw what I had to work with:

♠ A 9 6 5
♡ Q 7 5 2
♢ 10 5 4
♣ K 7

```
    N
W       E
    S
```

♠ J 4 3 2
♡ A 9 6
♢ A 9 8
♣ A 5 4

West	North	East	South
#≌p7	Shoolah	Spillane	Me
pass	pass	1♡	dbl
2♣	dbl	pass	2♠
all pass			

Aliens | 103 |

Odd he didn't simply bid his spades. He certainly wasn't a hand hog. Did he play them badly?

East inserted the ten after I called for the five and I won the ace. You don't make money taking saves against two diamonds, so it behooved me to make something of this uninspired collection.

Another round, if you please, the booming, mellifluous voice came again.

I chuckled uneasily under my breath, hoping this was merely my sophomoric sense of humor coming to the fore. It might have been, except...

Leading hearts right back had a lot to be said for it. I had the spots to set up my queen eventually, but I didn't have time to draw trumps and use it before they switched to diamonds and a pitch became meaningless. Having Stinky ruff out the queen on the fourth round while I got rid of a diamond was no big deal and could work out quite nicely if he was ruffing from a doubleton or tripleton honor. A tripleton would be a ruff from a natural; a doubleton would allow me to drop his honor and then lead through East up to my otherwise useless jack.

Quite the pair of coincidences. They made it decidedly harder to take what I was devoutly hoping were manifestations of my genius at face value. Keep the weirdness stuffed in the trunk. *Voodoo wouldn't still be around without the power of suggestion,* I hastened to remind myself.

With a trepidation unrelated to the play, I placed the nine of hearts on the table. Stinky surprised me by playing the three. Nobody plays four-card majors anymore. I think Kantar was two hundred when he died and even he had given up on them. East apparently was going for a lead-director, which was good news: he'd probably opened light and that meant West *could* be ruffing from something useful.

East eyed me coolly after he won his jack, and produced the two of diamonds.

Whoopsie. Someone knew that two people playing the same suit can both be wrong, but they can't both be right. I had been mired so deeply in my clever plan and in my extraneous thoughts that the monkey wrench caught me flat-footed. I dithered sufficiently before

I ducked for everyone to know I wasn't deciding whether to claim. Stinky won the jack and returned the three to Spillane's queen and my ace.

I cogitated. Not much. There was only way out. I played my top clubs, ruffed the third round in dummy to clean things up, then set aside my atheism for a moment and called for the ten of diamonds.

My luck was in. East played low and Stinky won. This was the ending:

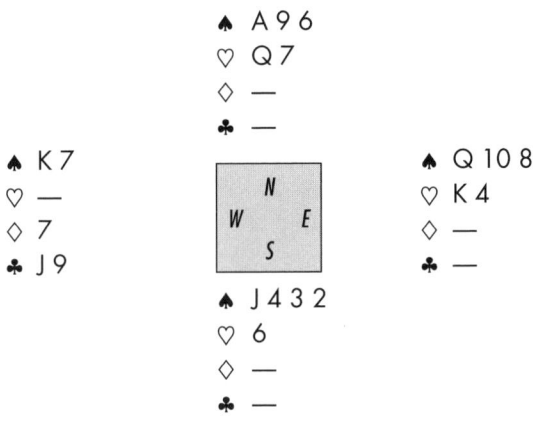

```
                 ♠ A 9 6
                 ♡ Q 7
                 ◇ —
                 ♣ —
  ♠ K 7                         ♠ Q 10 8
  ♡ —            N              ♡ K 4
  ◇ 7         W     E           ◇ —
  ♣ J 9          S              ♣ —
                 ♠ J 4 3 2
                 ♡ 6
                 ◇ —
                 ♣ —
```

Stinky had no choice but to try a spade, but I popped the ace and led one right back. Well, not *right* back; I don't play the game just for money. I dragged it out so he had time to fully appreciate the horror of what might unfold. Give him credit. When it did and he had to apply the coup-de-grace to his side by giving me my ruff-sluff to take care of my heart loser, he retained his neutral orange. East had to look on helplessly with his high trump — he too gave no sign of his agitation — as a club got led. The whole deal:

Aliens

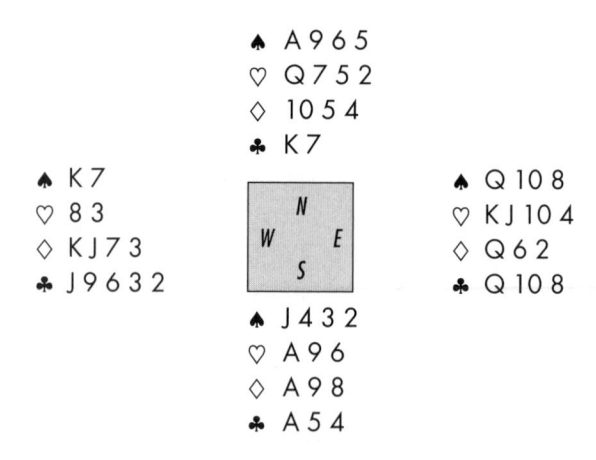

```
            ♠ A 9 6 5
            ♡ Q 7 5 2
            ◇ 10 5 4
            ♣ K 7
♠ K 7                          ♠ Q 10 8
♡ 8 3          N               ♡ K J 10 4
◇ K J 7 3    W   E             ◇ Q 6 2
♣ J 9 6 3 2    S               ♣ Q 10 8
            ♠ J 4 3 2
            ♡ A 9 6
            ◇ A 9 8
            ♣ A 5 4
```

This was not Stinky's night. He could have returned his king of diamonds originally instead of a low one, so it would have been East and his king of hearts getting in the third time around. Exiting with the spade king would also have been an improvement, though a *pro forma* one in this case; no way would I have played him for king-queen doubleton. I gulped at this point, realizing I had been playing with fire. What if he had deemed his error, the one I had so relished grinding into him, egregious enough to warrant his demise? I would have been collateral damage. *That was one base the horoscope didn't cover*, I thought darkly.

Everyone politely tossed their cards to Shoolah, who had some difficulty scraping them up and dealing with his three-fingered claws. I wondered how his species had managed to evolve with such poorly adapted tool-using appendages.

His labor was not in vain. It produced this fistful:

```
♠ K Q 10 8 7 4
♡ K
◇ A K
♣ A 8 7 4
```

Wow. The card gods were genuinely feeling guilty, I thought with the sense of entitlement of the truly egocentric. The auction began, surprisingly, 'One heart' on my right, an annoying complication I couldn't seriously complain about. I doubled as unexuberantly as I could. No

| 106 | Bridge Mix

sooner was the bid out of my mouth than I realized East had opened out of turn. Stinky and partner seemed unperturbed by the turn of events. It went a quick 'pass, pass'.

Pass? I had the king of hearts and partner was penalty passing? East apparently believed us, because he bailed with an SOS redouble. I passed, curious as to what Elysian fields they might gambol into. Stinky tried two diamonds, which looked like the least of their evils from my hand, and partner and East passed smoothly. I bid three spades — never cuebid in a pick-up game — and North took me seriously enough to bounce me to six. I wanted to bid seven, but I also wanted to ensure a decent meal, so I passed. Stinky had a heart to lead — the three — and partner and I did our ritual exchange. My eyebrows grazed my hairline, my needler forgotten, when I saw his cards. I didn't see his initial reaction, but his eyes had narrowed and he was looking sideways at Spillane as he handed my cards back. This was why:

♠ A 6 5
♡ A Q J 10 4 2
♢ 10
♣ Q 6 2

♠ K Q 10 8 7 4
♡ K
♢ A K
♣ A 8 7 4

West	North	East	South
#≅p7	Shoolah	Spillane	Me
		1♡	dbl
pass	pass	redbl	pass
2♢	pass	pass	3♠
pass	6♠	all pass	

Aliens | 107 |

Give East full marks; a successful first-seat psych in second seat is an awesome display of table presence. He'd kept us out of seven in three different strains. I don't know why I assumed he'd known what he was doing, but I did. There was just something about him. I wondered if North had noticed the infraction at all. He certainly wouldn't have cared.

I was about to call for a small heart to make sure they ran — I got as far as 'Sm...' — when I heard an interior *Another round, if you please.*

This was alarming for two reasons: the exponential spike in bizarreness and the stupidity I had almost committed. It says a lot about me and my Scottish ancestry that I ranked them as near equals. The stupidity could have cost me money. Blown my wee brainies out, as Gray would have put it. If I'd won in hand, the only way back to dummy was spades; if those were 4-0, I would have screwed myself. I don't enjoy that, at the table.

This one was right out of the book. I didn't need hearts to run; I just needed three more tricks from them. If I took the simple precaution of swallowing the king with the ace and then kept going with the aforementioned — *shudder* — round of hearts, who cared if West ruffed? That would mean there *were* only three trumps left.

I recanted somberly and called for the ace. I was sweating at my close call despite the chill of the air conditioning. Humans are also the hothouse flowers of the Galaxy.

Virtue was rewarded:

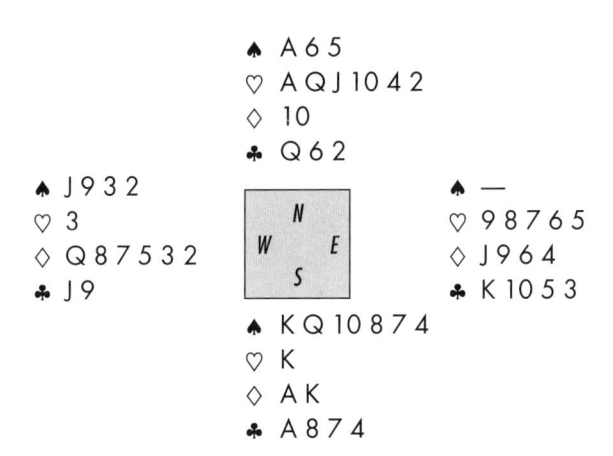

```
              ♠ A 6 5
              ♥ A Q J 10 4 2
              ◊ 10
              ♣ Q 6 2
♠ J 9 3 2                        ♠ —
♥ 3          ┌─────────┐         ♥ 9 8 7 6 5
◊ Q 8 7 5 3 2│    N    │         ◊ J 9 6 4
♣ J 9        │ W     E │         ♣ K 10 5 3
             │    S    │
             └─────────┘
              ♠ K Q 10 8 7 4
              ♥ K
              ◊ A K
              ♣ A 8 7 4
```

Elation buoyed me for the few seconds that passed until I recalled the prompting responsible for it. A swirling fog of doubt and ambiguity and not a little outright fear moved in to replace it. My fingers alone were able to muster the will to troop out of it and genuflect to pick up freshly dealt cards — hand-sized, from Spillane — and fan them. Only then did the rest of me follow — partway — and try to absorb what they were offering up to me:

```
              ♠ Q 8 2
              ♥ A 3 2
              ◊ 6 3 2
              ♣ K 6 3 2
```

Not up to snuff, I reflected absently, but when East passed — legitimately — I was relieved not have a decision to make. *Not a good sign.* Another generous slug of scotch blurred the sharp jangling in my brain. Stinky likewise downed more of his drink and burbled 'Two spades'. Partner doubled and East passed. On automatic pilot, I made the bid in front of my nose, and after Stinky's pass partner raised to three notrump. Stinky had the queen of hearts on the table the instant I passed. Partner bedecked the table with:

Aliens | 109 |

♠ K 10 3
♡ K 7 4
♢ A J 5 4
♣ A Q 7

```
    N
W       E
    S
```

♠ Q 8 2
♡ A 3 2
♢ 6 3 2
♣ K 6 3 2

West	North	East	South
#≚p7	Shoolah	Spillane	Me
		pass	pass
2♠	dbl	pass	2NT
pass	3NT	all pass	

I noted in passing that Stinky was probably tired of being on lead. I played small, eight —

Another round, if you please. Imperious.

It isn't up to me, I retorted angrily as I underplayed with my two. I caught myself up short, looked around guiltily. At least it appeared I hadn't blurted it out. Stinky continued hearts, as per — *shudder* — instructions.

I was now completely at a loss to rationalize this latest... what? A mating of astronomically odds-against chance and convergent suggestibility couldn't cut it. I flashed on Gray's haunted expression, looked at the scotch in front of me. Did something like this ever happen to him? It was Halloween, my birthday and the day of this inexplicable behavior. Unless there was some sort of psychosis time bomb that ticked away in families and struck precisely one day of the year, there was only one explanation. But, Occam's razor be damned, I could *not* accept the idea of supernatural intervention either. The Universe going crazy was no more plausible than a hypothetical Halloween fruitcake gene.

Which left me nowhere.

Stomach again came to my rescue. This time it was my brain that got bitch-slapped and ordered to focus. Sometimes it's good to be in the hands of a lower power. With the aid of the last of the scotch, my tilt-a-whirl of emotions stabilized to the point where I could bring myself back online. I looked at the board morosely.

Wa-a-ait a minute... Was ducking the heart any sort of masterstroke? Why, it was downright dangerous, I realized with the tiniest, most wishful seedling of hope. How would I have liked the ten of diamonds getting shoved through dummy's tenuous holding? Clubs could split and I still could have ended up going down in a cold contract. That plummy foghorn in my head would have been out to lunch then, wouldn't it?

I knew I was throwing myself a bone, and I had no intention of examining how valid my caviling was until much, much later, but for the moment I became a little less stressed about externals. A fallible voice in my head was a lot easier to deal with. And, divorced from it, the hands could revert to a singular series of flukes. Yessiree bob, they could.

I finally won the heart king in dummy — the entire table was getting fidgety — as East completed his high-low. I led a low spade off dummy and East of all people played the ace, which explained why Stinky hadn't wrestled with his choice of lead. The ten of hearts got returned to my ace, Stinky playing low. That was one suit counted.

I concentrated mightily, trying to lose myself in the cards. If clubs behaved, I had nine tricks. Could they? Stinky had ten major cards. If clubs were 3-3, fine. If they weren't, East would be in on the fourth one. That wouldn't do me any good if he had another club to cash, so he couldn't have more than four of those. Since he would be down to all diamonds, the question then became what honors did he have? If he had the king-queen, I didn't need to do anything. If he didn't have the king-queen, Stinky's singleton would be an honor and I would have to cash the ace before exiting with a club.

Galactic Standard is closely adhered to in rubber bridge. No Little Major crap. (Don't bother looking that up.) Take the bidding chaos involved when dealing with humans, multiply it by several orders of magnitude, and you can see why. Unless Stinky had gone completely out on a limb, he had a diamond honor to bring him up to the mandated 6-10 point range. (At the back of my mind I acknowledged all this meant that ducking the heart *had* been perfectly safe, but I pretended not to hear myself.)

I cashed the queen and king of spades, and East dumped diamonds. Then I cashed the ace-queen of clubs and exhaled when everyone showed in. When I cashed the diamond ace, Stinky showed in with the king:

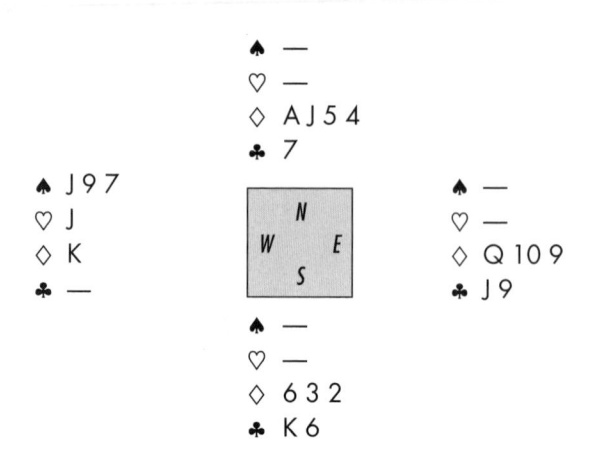

```
              ♠ —
              ♡ —
              ♢ A J 5 4
              ♣ 7
♠ J 9 7                    ♠ —
♡ J         N              ♡ —
♢ K       W   E            ♢ Q 10 9
♣ —         S              ♣ J 9
              ♠ —
              ♡ —
              ♢ 6 3 2
              ♣ K 6
```

Smugly, I came back to my club king and exited with the six to a plainly disgusted East.

The whole deal:

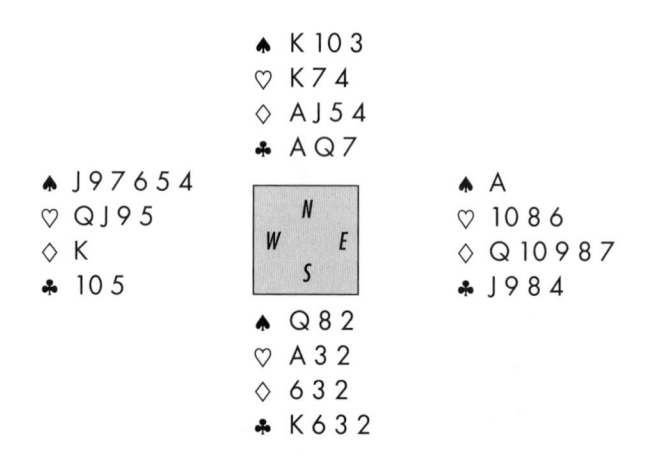

```
              ♠ K 10 3
              ♡ K 7 4
              ♢ A J 5 4
              ♣ A Q 7
♠ J 9 7 6 5 4              ♠ A
♡ Q J 9 5     N            ♡ 10 8 6
♢ K         W   E          ♢ Q 10 9 8 7
♣ 10 5        S            ♣ J 9 8 4
              ♠ Q 8 2
              ♡ A 3 2
              ♢ 6 3 2
              ♣ K 6 3 2
```

| 112 | *Bridge Mix*

'Please excuse me,' Shoolah suddenly announced in his ticked-off-cobra hiss. 'An urgent matter has just now come up.' He looked directly at me with lambent eyes. 'It concerns one who is an old friend of the family. Our time together is running out.' With this bombshell, he unilaterally dismissed himself and rose to clomp unceremoniously toward the exit.

I wanted to tackle him and drag him back to the table. Lest you think too ill of me, it wasn't because he was selfishly deserting me for a dying friend in the middle of my hot streak. Honestly. I was scared. My enforced truce with my doubts and fears not withstanding, I desperately needed to derail this train of coincidences. I needed a reality fix, a deal where no voice bellowed instructions at me, and I couldn't get that if we stopped. I didn't care if I got doubled and went for billions, as long as my head was empty (you know what I mean). Maybe the next deal would be the one. Classic addict rationalization, but we're talking about reality here.

A cold, antiseptic ice pick stabbed into my squirming panic. *How could he know about his friend?*

All communication devices were strictly policed during a game by the AIs to prevent information from spy devices or kibitzers being relayed to players. Humans do not have a lock on sleaze. Invisibly tiny recording motes hovering around the table made the AI adept at spotting visual signals too, so if anybody nearby as much as picked their — anything — to indicate somebody's club holding, they'd be busted. Rigellan waiters make excellent bouncers.

'He's a telepath,' Spillane informed me matter-of-factly. Apparently, I *had* started to converse with myself out loud.

A telepath. Of course he hadn't used his own voice! Everything suddenly started to fit, like when you run video backwards and the pieces of a broken vase jump back together. I was watery with relief. Almost to the point of asking #≅p7 if he had a spare diaper thingy. 'But — But I didn't think there was such a thing!' I exclaimed happily. 'Why didn't you —'

'Because,' he chuckled, 'it only works within their own family — crèche-mates, breeding partners, long term adoptees. They can send, and over any distance, but they can't receive anything other than emotions if it isn't consciously transmitted. No all-access pass for poaching.'

Gahhh. That wasn't what I wanted to hear. I didn't want to be unceremoniously shoved back into a universe ruled by astrologers. Surely he had to be mistaken. Somehow I must have...

As I recommenced exchanging half-nelsons with my demons, frozen in place, Spillane stretched luxuriously and stood.

'He's been on the horn a lot lately,' he said by way of nothing in particular. I barely heard him, but he must have taken my vacant expression for puzzlement, because he explained: 'Touching minds. With his crèche-mates. Organizing. Some big gathering of the families is coming up and he's near the top of his hierarchy. The Kohms are one of the largest and most prestigious families.'

With that, he rose effortlessly and bade us a languid farewell. I followed suit, shakily. I suspected we were both fleeing Stinky. Instinct pointed me at the bar and I shambled in its direction, brain roiling. For some reason, I tapped my chrono to switch it from ship's time. It was still my birthday back on Earth. Thirty seconds to midnight, EST. A red dot pulsed in the corner, and I mechanically tapped again. An account update. I nodded appreciatively. At least now I could fill dear old tummy, drink myself into insensibility, and wake up with a nice hangover that would move all my other problems to the back burner. For once, I'd be glad they've never found a cure.

As if my brain wasn't crowded enough, another something weighed in, formless but insistent. It began nibbling at me, albeit not sharply; it was like being gummed by a piranha.

'Shoolah Kohms,' I said aloud, on purpose. Why did that sound familiar? *Oh well, it'll come to me.*

Weird Scenes Inside the Ol' Mind

The creature I thought of as Sydney Greenstreet loomed on my left, large and feline, not purring but seeming to. Across from me, a reincarnated Peter Lorre swayed gently in his ropy self-spun sling like a nightmarish orange caterpillar giving up the ghost in the strands of a jumbo spiderweb. It was a real stretch picturing him in place of the insectoid Caroller — eye-stalks and all — but there *had* been a touch of the cockroach about the man. It's what made his characters work. The permanent droop in one of the six eye-stalks had given me a starting point.

It was easier to picture the imposing smooth-furred, wide-muzzled Brog as Sydney. Both had an air of well-fed benevolence, although in the Brog's case it wasn't transparently cultivated; he really was a big pussycat.

To my right, Mary Astor — delicate, wounded — Sydney's partner of the moment, was perched on her smoothly contoured formchair, multi-faceted almond eyes glittering like quartz crystals in the room's barely adequate indirect lighting. Remembering her real name would have been pointless anyway; it was ridiculously long and way too hard on my vocal cords to ever use. She was a Drehm ('*Have you ever seen a Drehm waaalking?*' kept playing in my head. I'd known I was going to regret thinking of it) and I gave her the part because she too belonged to dark and mysterious places; her still young homeworld was shrouded in a constant twilight where she and her kind soared on restless eternal winds above cruel canyons and ash-spewing volcanoes. She was two-thirds Sydney's size, though still a head (human) taller than me, and her arms were proportionately longer, as were the projecting triangular caves of her ears. But if you ignored those unnatural eyes, in profile the two of them could have been brother and sister. Had I not already assigned them their roles they would have been Thing One and Thing

Two. (Just to be clear, I'm a Seussophile, not a racist.) They had the same tawny fur, same finely molded felid skulls, deep chests, and powerful arm and legs with the same number of articulations. It was a slap in the face to convergent evolution because it was pure happenstance. Not only were the worlds that had originally spawned their kind thousands of light years apart — hers stuck up in a globular cluster, his cozy in the Hub — his was cool primordial savannah nourished, albeit sparingly, by a red dwarf star, a near-immortal sun. Grazing lands as opposed to aerial hunting grounds. Twice Earth gravity versus Mars gravity. Digging and harvesting claws versus grasping talons.

Her solidity was, however, an illusion. I could have lifted her with one arm. Her skeleton was carbon-fiber tubes that doubled as blood conduits. Some amazing evolution there. The ultra-light, ultra-strong framework allowed her arms and their expandable flight membranes to beat her homeworld's renegade winds into submission, winds that would have snapped an eagle's bones. The membranes too were a polymer, a dark gray weave veined with emerald and laminated with a shimmering transparency. Whenever she turned toward me, she was closer to two-dimensional than three; wind resistance demands streamlining. Edge-on, she was easy to lose against the background of beige alcoves and ornamental pillars across the room.

I like to romanticize these non-FTL intra-system short-hoppers as tramp steamers, like in the old movies I've been watching way too many of. A place where everyone has their stories, their dark secrets. Some of my fellow travelers would be fleeing life, some the law; others would be down on their luck or, like me, broken and drifting. Prime candidates, to a *noir* addict, for the French Foreign Legion. Not Mary, naturally, but you get the idea. In reality — not something I trust anymore — the ship was as romantic as a commuter train. It was basically a cargo shuttle with modular passenger quarters installed whenever the Rigellan consortium running it couldn't scrape up a full load.

I was the only one of the twenty or so on board to come close to actually fitting the criteria for *noir*dom. Bogie in a purple zoot suit and big-brimmed fedora. From what I'd overhead so far in the five-day, three-stop trip, the others were mainly business drones — literally, in one case — and bureaucrats. No leavening of artists or entertainers. No leisure classes. One intensely boring proselytizing priest from someplace that hadn't yet outgrown religion, and a probable crime boss and his two minions — not as titillating as you might think. Criminal enterprise is alive and well most everywhere among us younger species, but it's virtually all gray-collar (like white, only dirty). Rubbing somebody out is a real career ender; you have to disappear into a non-Conglomerate world or you *will* get nailed and brain-fried. Nobody wants to spend his prolonged life hiding out on a pre-industrial backwater.

The moderate number of braided filaments crowning Lorre's head-segment (not 'Peter' — that's someone you would feel comfortable leaving your children with) marked him as a mid-level government functionary. He was only the second of his species I'd run into and I'd fallen into the trap of asking him if he knew #≅p7, before remembering that was like him asking me if I knew Brad. However, he'd acknowledged that he did know of him, but that #≅p7 was way above his pay grade. It caused me to wondered if his predecessor's incongruously vulpine head-segment was considered aristocratic, since p*3's was an unremarkable flat-featured adjunct to his reedy eye-stalks, a chitinous slab.

Mary (I only had pronoun reference to go by for her sex; the unadorned magenta harness criss-crossing her chest was unisex) was a cosmetics distributor. *There's* a commonality you wouldn't expect. It's not universal, but nearly. The bright red sample case sitting upright beside her on the crazy-quilt flooring must have been opened recently; a smell like a lilac-scented hyena's armpit clung to it. I found it disturbingly arousing. Some pheromone in there was awfully close to human.

As for Sydney, I had no idea what a Founder was doing on a milk run (like a beer run, only slower for some reason) out on the Rim. Laying aside my normal cynicism for a second, it was a genuine honor to be sitting next to one of his kind. Awkward though. Would you really want, say, the Buddha in your foursome when you're trying to carve out your opponents' hearts?

It has been an unpleasant year. Ever since Halloween. Since I found out who Sherlock Holmes was — or actually *wasn't*. Who his boon companion was. I haven't turned to (more correctly, returned to) drugs or alcohol, not because of iron will but because I don't have the credit; I've barely been keeping my head above water, financially or emotionally. The upside of the resultant dieting is that my potbelly has remained merely adorable despite my strict regimen of moping. I can't seem to concentrate like I used to. I haven't descended into pigeonhood, but neither have I been much of a pigeon hawk. My play has become... hawkward? I didn't trust myself in high-stakes games anymore. Which is why I was reduced to taking passage on this bucket of tachyons. I called it that, but it was reasonably spacious and pleasant, just far less ritzy than what I had been accustomed to. Unlike with the big inter-system luxury liners, there were never more than days between ports of call instead of weeks. Without the corresponding easy lucre from the idle rich, it was hard scrabbling, but I didn't need to score big to survive, which was all I was up to doing. And I was too out of shape and too squeamish to be hustling my sorry, sagging ass, even if any of the life-forms on this ark of the convenient craved some strange.

Did I mention it was Halloween once again — my birthday? Heroically, I had refused to stay curled up into a fetal ball in my room to wait it out with a bottle of scrounged rotgut. I'd prepared, though. I had read every horoscope I could find on the Skein to fortify myself with a healthy concentration of contradictory absurdity. Terran newspapers were naturally the only ones to carry them and there were only four, though those were heavily syndicated. They were still in their traditional spot on the back pages with bridge columns and obituaries. Their survival speaks volumes about us; the ancients had an excuse, but nowadays, when people can be born *in* their sign... And if that included the locals, you could have entire systems chock full of Aquarians. Not much scope for a pick-up line there.

We had been at it for an hour in one of those arduous rubbers where you build skyscrapers above the line, and so far — fingers crossed — nothing astrologically applicable had come up. If it did, with no Heeby-Jeeby around, it would be very bad news. Much as I disliked the idea of someone running around inside my head and yelling at me, and impossible though that was supposed to be, I had formed an uneasy truce with it. This ongoing nebulousness had become reflected in my life for the past year, but as long as I maintained my gentleman's agreement not to question the explanation too closely, it served to stave off the question of the Supernatural's involvement. The initial blowback from The Adventure of the Paradoxical Alien had initially swamped my inability to explain the insidious relevance of the instigating horoscope, but a niggling little worm of suspicion had returned soon after and wouldn't crawl away. Sure, if the Crusaders could turn 'Love thy neighbor' into 'Kill all heathens', finding a hint of relevance in a vague and all-purpose pearl of wisdom wasn't hard — but I was counting the minutes to midnight, when I could declare myself Supernatural-free. *Like there's a statute of limitations*, I snarked. Well, I could at least consign it to the oubliette where I kept childhood horrors and those perpetrated by suspicious customs agents unfamiliar with human anatomy. I could get on with my life.

Another hour to go. Coincidentally we were also docking around then at someplace whose name escaped me. My itinerary wasn't something I cared about.

Lorre machine-gunned cards at us, six snaky upper arms blurring. In short order I picked up:

♠ A J 8 6
♡ K
♢ Q 10 7 6 4
♣ J 8 2

Not horrible, but after partner buzzed a pass, Mary silenced me with a squeaky one diamond and they played patty-cake via one heart, one spade, one notrump, two notrump, three notrump. Partner flicked the seven of spades into this:

```
                    ♠ K Q 10 9
         N          ♥ A 9 4
     W       E      ♦ K 5 3
         S          ♣ Q 4 3

         ♠ A J 8 6
         ♥ K
         ♦ Q 10 7 6 4
         ♣ J 8 2
```

West	North	East	South
Sydney	Lorre	Mary	Me
	pass	1♦	pass
1♥	pass	1♠	pass
1NT	pass	2NT	pass
3NT	all pass		

Sydney — whose name had flown right by me in my starstruck paralysis when Lorre, a fellow lounge habitué, had introduced us — didn't pause before calling for the ten, and I won the jack as he followed small. Figuring this one rated to expire from natural causes, I returned a passive eight of clubs, not hankering to do anything egregiously stupid in such exalted company. He was ready with the ace, and partner's five wasn't enthusiastic, but when I won the next spade, I decided to continue my relentless assault. Declarer won his king, went to the club queen — partner having contributed the six and ten — to cash the remaining spades, pitching low hearts both times, while partner pitched one. Then he called for a diamond. Mary obliged, and I played the four, him the nine, partner the ace.

Yes. I had been hornswoggled. This was what I was now looking at:

```
              ♠ —
   ┌─────┐   ♡ A 9 4
   │  N  │   ◇ K 5
   │W   E│   ♣ —
   │  S  │
   └─────┘
♠ —
♡ K
◇ Q 10 7 6
♣ —
```

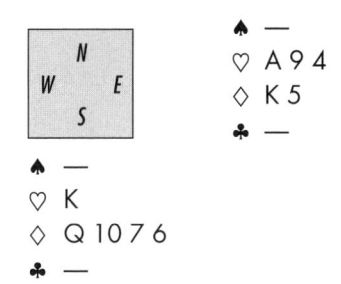

Sweat beaded my forehead as I looked at my king of hearts. *Oh, crap.* One of the horoscopes had said: 'A big heart can be a liability.' I wasn't prepared to have it sneak up on me like this. Where was the *sturm und drang* this time? The timely *sturm und drang* — the clarion voice in my head, the sudden insight. At least the bloody intrusive things had been useful before, even if their presentation had scared me to death. I didn't know what to make of this after-the-fact portentousness.

Being miffed was, of course, an act. It didn't fool the tiny hairs on the back of my neck. Or the ones pushing against the inside of my sleeves like when the air is ionizing before a thunderstorm. Mind you, the horoscope had added, 'But don't let it discourage you.' It didn't help much. Rotgut and snuggling dust bunnies under my bed had been the way to go after all.

I traded my foreboding for a terror to be named later and returned resignedly to my real-world predicament. It was akin to forcing yourself out of an unpleasant dream — say, a naked-on-the-street one — to find you're in a badly leaking lifeboat. It wasn't hard to visualize what was coming next and it wasn't going to be pretty. For me.

Sure enough, partner skewered me with the inevitable heart. The queen, to be exact. Declarer adroitly ducked to my king, and I got to give him his ninth trick with his third jack of diamonds. Wow. He was wasted on 'Go Fish'.

This was the entire deal:

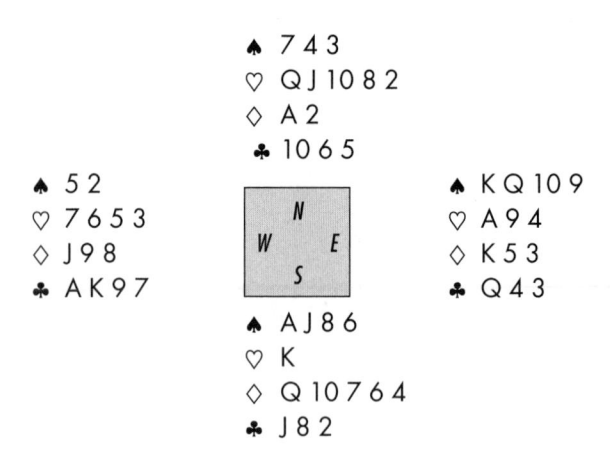

```
              ♠ 7 4 3
              ♥ Q J 10 8 2
              ◊ A 2
              ♣ 10 6 5
  ♠ 5 2                          ♠ K Q 10 9
  ♥ 7 6 5 3      N               ♥ A 9 4
  ◊ J 9 8      W   E             ◊ K 5 3
  ♣ A K 9 7      S               ♣ Q 4 3
              ♠ A J 8 6
              ♥ K
              ◊ Q 10 7 6 4
              ♣ J 8 2
```

My shortsightedness was typical of me lately. Declarer had been insanely devious, but it would only have worked against an idiot. If it had been possible for me to actually *see* his four club tricks, even in my fugue state I might have glommed on to the fact that the ace of diamonds would give him nine tricks, and dutifully gone up queen, thus preventing the Moron's Fork Coup. Of course, it was only the last gaffe of several. Ducking the first spade would have left us in charge no matter what he did, and switching to a diamond or a heart at any stage would obviously have saved me from being so thoroughly embarrassed (from the Latin for 'without pants').

That was the inglorious end of my stint with Lorre. Despite the last deal, I was about even. I hadn't completely sucked and I'd had the cards to do better, but this crew was sharper than most. Lorre, not so much, though he had his moments. I think the number of tumblers of lumpy purple liquid he usually disposed of was responsible for his in-and-out play. The Brog were tipplers extraordinaire, especially when it came to 'Go Fish' — go figure — but not at the bridge table and not when doing something equally serious, like governing their Empire or co-administering the Conglomerate that has kept the peace since forever. Perhaps the fact that they found poker too confrontational was a hint as to why their diplomatic skill was legendary.

Us humans are still the benchmark when it comes to cards though, and I was letting down the side.

Mary and Lorre switched. The three-meter-high gooseneck standard that suspended his sling rotated smoothly to its new position.

Chairs weren't much use to a species that didn't bend in the middle; tying shoes was the province of the three heavy-duty pairs of thick lifting arms cantilevered out of the lower part of his thorax's light orange enamel like rust-covered waldoes.

Mary stepped out of the way with surprising nimbleness considering the ship's Rigellan gravity was more than twice what she was used to. She also hefted her sample case easily. Her pale aqua formchair (trust a female; us males hadn't bothered to change the black default setting) melted back into the deck and reappeared in its new place.

Sydney stood and stretched like any cat, only vertically. His retractable claws eased out to full scythe length, as long as my forearm. He — females were the splashy peacocks of the species — had no clothes but he wasn't naked. His 'fur' was a symbiote, a fungoid carpet that provided insulation and a degree of protection in return for a free lunch. It had no neural connection to him and it was only attached to the leathery skin underneath by a layer of osmotic mucus, so it could be slit painlessly (for him) and peeled off. A quick shower and it was time to hit the beach. His covering could have been tens of thousands of years old, since it was traditionally inherited — kept in a nutrient bath and parceled out to newborns. Yuckiest hand-me-downs ever.

I squirmed around a little, but couldn't get very comfortable. My formchair couldn't quite get it right. The table's height made me feel like a kid in a highchair anyway, but the formchairs on this ship were so old their programming didn't include humans, so they used a race with my approximate dimensions for a template and they gave me a mid-range wedgie (school had made me somewhat of an expert). I guess if you're dealing with aliens, anal probing of some sort is inevitable.

We cut for deal in the new rotation and Lorre got to do it again. With fresh determination to face whatever came my way, and to gain back some face, I picked up:

♠ Q 10 6 4
♡ A Q 7 4
♢ A 5 2
♣ 5 4

The finely barbed black fingery things at the ends of Lorre's middle pair of serpentine upper arms did his sorting and then sharply folded and unfolded the cards. Evidently his attempt to *shazam* them into an upgrade failed, because he chittered a quick pass.

I opened a club. Let those of you who are without sin cast the first stone. I wasn't usually this cute, but right then I had an acute need to assert more external control to counterbalance the way I was treading quicksand internally. Mind you, I wasn't so needy that I wouldn't have opened a weak notrump if I had noticed that I'd counted my ace of hearts at least twice. Talk about not having it together.

Sydney doubled, partner bid a diamond, Lorre let it go, and I carried on my campaign of disingenuousness (lying, with a B.A.) with one notrump. I didn't like my seventeen points well enough to stretch to two notrump. Partner invited, and that's when a recount turned up the reason I hadn't liked them. How had I ever thought this crap could add up to that much? I passed serenely, a triumph of will marred by a slight tremor in my hands.

I couldn't tell if I was imagining it, but there seemed to be a break in tempo in Sydney's pass.

When he dropped the two of spades delicately on the table, Mary put her cards face-down and gestured she wanted to see mine, something she hadn't done with Sydney. I didn't proffer them right away, hoping she might take the hint. She either ignored me or couldn't read the mannerism, because she leaned forward and her elongated paw-fingers lifted the cards deliberately from my clutches. Her light-scattering eyes and the shimmering cape formed by her extended bat wing suddenly looked very Halloweenish. The eyes regarded my offering unreadably, but the round table's transparent top allowed me to see her retractable talons make an appearance. They were right wicked-looking. I busied myself not making eye contact when she handed my cards back, slowly. Her jaws opened slightly. *My, Grandma, what sharp dentures.*

I half-expected her to fling her hand down, but she laid it out methodically. It was better than I deserved:

♠ 5 3
♡ 8 5 3
♢ K J 10 9 8
♣ A 3 2

```
    N
W       E
    S
```

♠ Q 10 6 4
♡ A Q 7 4
♢ A 5 2
♣ 5 4

West	North	East	South
Sydney	Mary	Lorre	Me
			1♣
dbl	1♢	pass	1NT
pass	2NT	all pass	

Opposite a supposed 15-17 points, I've found a jump to game with her hand to be winning strategy, especially vulnerable. After all, game had some sort of play opposite my crap, and I was a king shy of a minimum. Plus, confident bidding is far less likely to attract a speculative double. I couldn't blame her though; she'd seen me defend the last deal. It went low, jack, and I won my queen. Odd lead. Who leads away from fourth ace-king?

Whatever his reasons, I knew I didn't lust after a spade back through me if the diamond hook lost to one of East's meager store of face cards. In a fit of what I hoped was inspiration, I went to the diamond king — prompting the standard flurry of high spots — and ran the jack. Don't roll your eyes. There was a method in my madness. Half-assed, but a method. At worst I was taking a step on the road to actual thought.

When Sydney won his queen (*sigh*) he turned her over and pulled out the farthest card on the left. I had no ethical qualms about filing that away. It was the club king. Rats. I'd been slightly hopeful my one

Weird Scenes Inside the Ol' Mind

club opening would scare him off. But, predictably, it was a pipe dream against somebody who knew what he was doing. It wasn't a deep dark secret that diamonds were blocked. I ducked and Lorre encouraged with the nine. Sydney followed up with the queen. I ducked again. He persevered with the ten. Imagine the look on his face — never mind, it didn't mean anything to me either — when I showed out and ditched my ace of diamonds. My half-assed fallback had come through.

I got down to the business of running diamonds. Naturally West had started with a doubleton queen. He pitched the nine of hearts, then the eight, then the seven of spades. I threw my low hearts and East helped me out by dumping the missing clubs, so West was revealed to have been 4-4 in the majors with three clubs. He was down to a stiff A-K of spades and two hearts. Regardless of whether he had the heart king, I could just throw him in on a spade and let him lead into me. Sweet.

OTHERS DO NOT ALWAYS PUT FORTH THEIR BEST AROUND YOU. THE KEY TO SUCCESS IS TO UNDERSTAND WHY.

OmigodOmigodOmigod. It was back. The real deal. Louder than ever. What do I do What do I do Wha— *Not always... forth... best. Son of a bitch. He had five spades.*

Explosively decompressing from hyper-panic into relatively calm, self-contained enlightenment was like a souped-up version of having the stomach-churning dread of your promised encounter with the school bully disappear after the first punch. All I knew was the voice, with its familiar poncey accent, couldn't have been put into my head via an inexplicable telepathy this time. No telepath, no telepathy. I could feel the Supernatural's walled-off presence limbering up in the bullpen. It had been patiently riding the bench for the better part of a year now and it was sensing a chance to get in the game. Before it could, I reconsidered a really low draft choice that I'd never given any playing time.

Schizophrenia. Why, I reasoned (let's call it that) not call it up from the minors? Never mind that an annual one-night-only outbreak was... implausible. Maybe the last time had just been a try-out, and now it was going to stick. I was okay with that. They have good drugs for it. I could get better. Besides, a separate personality talking to me, even if it was sharper as well as being condescending about it, was still me, right? I'd always wanted a brother. And if he helped me win a lot of credits, I could get him drunk and make him look foolish too.

As for the horoscope, well, here it got tricky... but the damned thing was anything but explicit. I'd pretty much cherry-picked meaning out of it; on some level, perhaps from that hitch before Sydney's final pass, I'd intuited something was off. When is a two not a fourth-best lead? Answer: when it's made by a sneaky alien. Of course he had had five spades; if he'd had four, he would never have pitched down to the stiff ace-king and two hearts. He would have kept all his spades and dared me to guess what to do about the heart king. Why hadn't he overcalled instead of doubling? Why, because he'd thought that sitting behind me made his hand too strong.

Schizophrenia, then. Maddening, because my auditory hallucination and I shared a subconscious, so why wasn't that communicating directly with me? A small price to pay, however, because the little hairs on my neck and arms stood down, warily. They bought it, for now.

I struck while the iron was hot — i.e., before I could think of more sports metaphors and before I began to *dwell* — to reconnect with the prosaic worry in front of me. Selective ADD is my most called-upon skill.

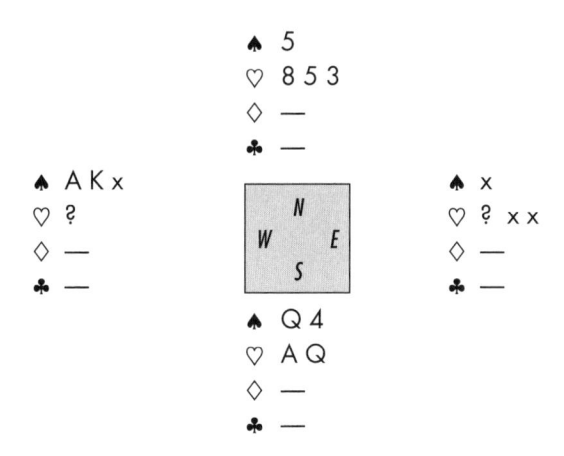

```
                ♠ 5
                ♡ 8 5 3
                ◇ —
                ♣ —
  ♠ A K x                       ♠ x
  ♡ ?          ┌─────┐          ♡ ? x x
  ◇ —          │  N  │          ◇ —
  ♣ —          │W   E│          ♣ —
               │  S  │
               └─────┘
                ♠ Q 4
                ♡ A Q
                ◇ —
                ♣ —
```

I backed my — you heard me — judgment and led a heart directly to my ace, with gratifyingly regicidal results.

The whole shebang:

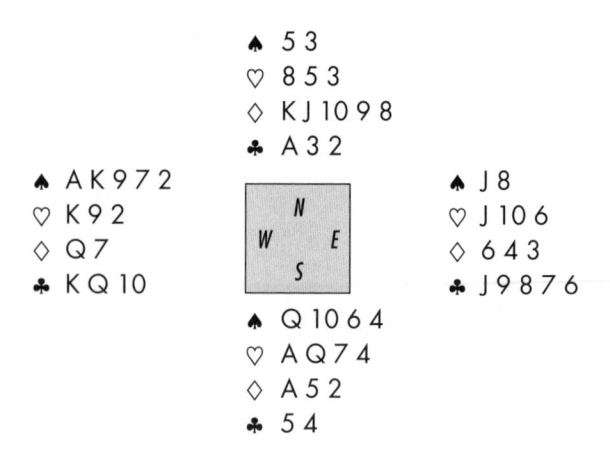

```
              ♠ 5 3
              ♥ 8 5 3
              ♦ K J 10 9 8
              ♣ A 3 2
♠ A K 9 7 2                    ♠ J 8
♥ K 9 2        N               ♥ J 10 6
♦ Q 7       W     E            ♦ 6 4 3
♣ K Q 10       S               ♣ J 9 8 7 6
              ♠ Q 10 6 4
              ♥ A Q 7 4
              ♦ A 5 2
              ♣ 5 4
```

I interrupted my triumphal parade down brain street — steadfastly not dwelling on who else might be on the float — to find I had shuffled and dealt on automatic pilot and everybody but me was sorting. I picked up my handiwork to find:

```
              ♠ J 7
              ♥ K 10 7 5 4
              ♦ A K Q 5
              ♣ 9 4
```

No cause for complaint here. I hoped I hadn't lost it to the extent that I had sworn myself to secrecy about slipping myself an extra ace or king. There was no overhead AI to catch it, but schizophrenia ('a voice in my head made me!') would have been a hard sell for creatures to whom the concept was almost certainly incomprehensible. It would have been a hard sell in Bedlam.

After my one-heart bid, Sydney rumble-purred a pass and partner squeaked out Blackwood. (*Not* keycard. The screw-up potential still limits it to experienced partnerships — who still screw it up.) Lorre clicked a pass. I dutifully bid five diamonds, Sydney passed, Mary checked for kings, thought for a while, and then jumped to seven hearts. Nobody sacrificed or doubled, and after I passed her over my cards, freely, and got them back without any talon play, Sydney put the nine of spades on the table, and what to my wondering eyes should appear but this:

♠ A K 6 5 2
♡ A Q 9
♢ 2
♣ A K 8 2

```
      N
  W       E
      S
```

♠ J 7
♡ K 10 7 5 4
♢ A K Q 5
♣ 9 4

West	North	East	South
Sydney	Mary	Lorre	Me
			1♡
pass	4NT	pass	5♢
pass	5NT	pass	6♡
pass	7♡	all pass	

She'd clearly been concerned about the new factor of my punch-drunk bidding on top of my erratic play. *Yeah, like you were a paragon of virtuous bidding last rubber*, I reminded her bravely, just not out loud.

I won the ace, Lorre dishing out the three. This rated to be as unchallenging as I'd hoped. Being a starving artist doesn't work for me; I need steak — even reconstituted — to do my best work. I cashed the ace of hearts, it being immune to ruffing. All cooperated, West with an ominous eight. At least he'd had one. Sure enough, when I cashed the queen, he pitched a club. So much for my diamond ruff. I wondered for a second if I could still do it if I organized a trump coup, but I had to put that on unpaid leave; Lorre would need four diamonds, and with four hearts his paucity of black cards would make cashing both black ace-kings more hazardous than I liked. Straightforwardly finessing his jack and drawing trumps was also unappetizing; spades would have to be 3-3 for my lone remaining trump to part them and get me to the promised land.

Weird Scenes Inside the Ol' Mind

ALWAYS REMEMBER HOW IMPORTANT LOVE IS. WHEN ALL ELSE FAILS IT WILL BE THERE.

I clutched at the table with my free hand and my cards with the other, sublimating the reflex to clap both hands over my ears. *Does it have to arrive with this drunk-on-the-next-barstool loudness?* I whined to myself. And, while I was kvetching, why so damned cryptic? *My skull's landlord wannabe is turning out to be more insufferable than me,* I blustered, working desperately to maintain the fiction. The irony that I was now griping about the very opaqueness that enabled me to rationalize the other horoscope away was not entirely lost on me. My telltale hairs stirred restlessly, but didn't stand at attention. I feared it was only because I couldn't see the horoscope's relevance.

A thought gonged. LOVE. Clyde? *Bridge Squeezes Complete?*

Petty annoyance momentarily masked the bitter blend of gratitude and hopelessness fomented by yet another tailored 'coincidence'. Recognition of the compound squeeze possibility should have been second nature (poor choice of words). What was wrong with me? It was like I'd spent the past year waiting to relapse into relying on these interjections to jump-start my thought processes.

I called upon my selective ADD yet again, and refocused. I had the main ingredient; I didn't have a recipe. (Does this make you miss the sports metaphors?) I can never remember Love's, amazingly concise though they are. I assure myself it's because school made me allergic to anything resembling rote learning.

I started by finessing East's heart jack, West letting go another club. When I drew the last heart, he threw a spade, and so did dummy. When I next led a spade, Sydney showed in with the nine. Were spades 3-3? Would that absolve the horoscope of responsibility? Hope flared. I called for the king — and East showed out with a diamond. Sneaky ol' Sydney had been at it again. *Sigh.* For a moment there, a relativistic universe had seemed possible again. *Just when I thought I was out... they pull me back in,* I Corleoned. Contract-wise it made no difference, I recognized at last. I could now just cash the ace of clubs — so I wouldn't have to count as high — and ruff a spade back to my hand with my last trump to manufacture the classic ending I should have visualized from the get-go:

```
        ♠ 6
        ♥ —
        ♦ 2
        ♣ K 8 2
♠ Q                          ♠ —
♥ —         N                ♥ —
♦ x x x x  W   E             ♦ x x
♣ —         S                ♣ Q 10 6
        ♠ —
        ♥ —
        ♦ A K Q 5
        ♣ 4
```

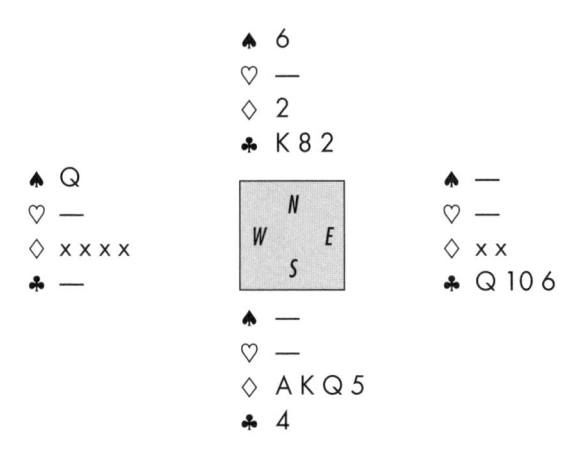

Notice I had unblocked my nine of clubs as a matter of sound technique. I always do things like that when it can't possibly matter.

Isn't the inexorability of the cards when everything comes together the main reason we play the game? It makes you feel the universe is a rational, ordered place, and that was especially soul-nurturing right then. The crushing of an opponent is merely an enjoyable side-effect. Unfortunately I wasn't in the mood to savor it. I led the nine of clubs and showed Sydney my diamonds. Torturing the Buddha would have been unseemly anyway, and besides, he was already folding his cards. He'd probably been resigned to it as soon as he saw his partner didn't have a trump trick. It made me long for the days when I was the smarty-pants at the table.

This was the entire deal:

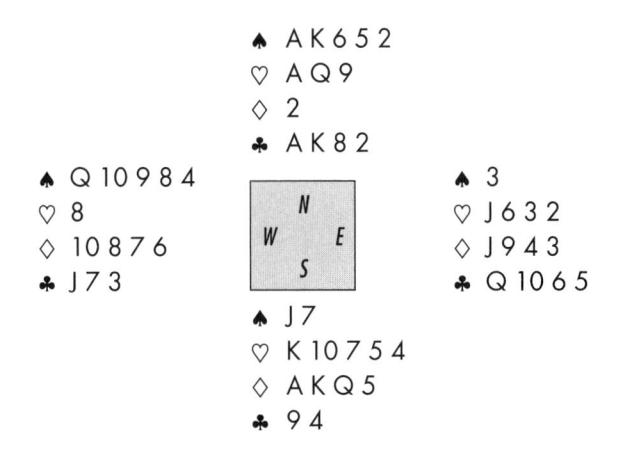

```
                ♠ A K 6 5 2
                ♥ A Q 9
                ♦ 2
                ♣ A K 8 2
♠ Q 10 9 8 4                    ♠ 3
♥ 8              N              ♥ J 6 3 2
♦ 10 8 7 6      W   E           ♦ J 9 4 3
♣ J 7 3          S              ♣ Q 10 6 5
                ♠ J 7
                ♥ K 10 7 5 4
                ♦ A K Q 5
                ♣ 9 4
```

Weird Scenes Inside the Ol' Mind

Fate had made darn sure it would get its pound of flesh. The deal was foolproof. I imagine you already noticed that if West and East had chosen to interchange the minors they guarded, the alternative ending would have been unchanged as far as my holdings went. If you were too riveted to think (boastful *and* diplomatic, a rare combination):

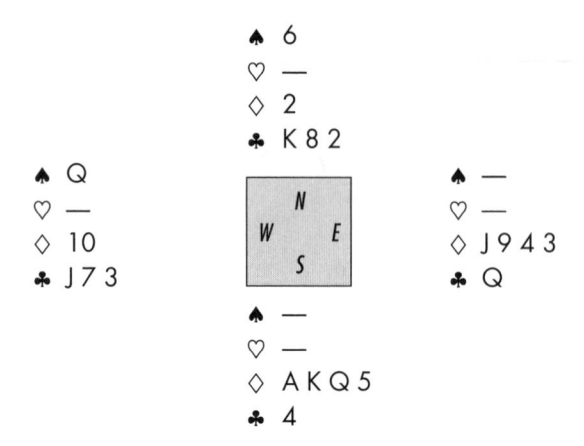

```
              ♠ 6
              ♡ —
              ♢ 2
              ♣ K 8 2
♠ Q                       ♠ —
♡ —           N           ♡ —
♢ 10        W   E         ♢ J 9 4 3
♣ J 7 3       S           ♣ Q
              ♠ —
              ♡ —
              ♢ A K Q 5
              ♣ 4
```

Now, cashing diamonds is what flattens West.

Horoscopes 3, peace of mind 0. Love, priceless.

Cards the size of dinner plates clumped in front of me, courtesy of Sydney, for the next deal. They reverted to a manageable size as I scooped them up and concentrated mightily on making the neatest fan of them ever. *Stay in limbo. Win now. Drink later.*

My make-work project revealed:

♠ Q J 9 4
♡ J 6 4 3
♢ 7 5
♣ A 9 8

Sydney passed. Mary opened one diamond, Lorre passed, and I bid one notrump. I couldn't help myself. It didn't even feel incorrigible by now. Partner jumped to three as I remembered I was going to have to fork over the evidence.

| 132 | Bridge Mix

I guess she was getting used to me or we hadn't missed a major-suit fit, because she didn't throw my cards back at me. Maybe she had a sense of humor. Anyhow, this was our ammunition:

♠ A 2
♡ A K 5
♢ A K 10 9 8 6 3
♣ 5

```
    N
 W     E
    S
```

♠ Q J 9 4
♡ J 6 4 3
♢ 7 5
♣ A 9 8

West	North	East	South
Sydney	Mary	Lorre	Me
pass	1♢	pass	1NT
pass	3NT	all pass	

Sydney led the two of clubs, most likely another lie given how many were out there. Diplomacy does require subterfuge, but I couldn't believe the Brog could practice it this indiscriminately and still be successful. Was he indulging himself a bit because this was after all a game, or had he been relegated out here to the hind end of nowhere because he was somebody's embarrassing nephew who needed to be put where he couldn't do much damage?

Too bad about the lead. The going-down-a-lot part now made three no much less attractive than five diamonds. Lorre played the king and I kissed my hand goodbye with the ace. Lousy technique, but again, it was a table control issue. Ducking, having them pounding clubs at me — in my fragile state it would have felt too much like being bullied. Sydney had the jack of diamonds on the table almost before I led one to the ace.

Unpropitious. However, I didn't have to rush into things. I cashed the ace-king of hearts and Sydney coughed up the queen on the second round, Lorre signaling with the ten and nine that I had fourth jack. *Hmm.* A hand entry. I now had the option of leading diamonds at the board one more time in case I wanted to get suckered into double-finessing when the bad ol' puddy tat was playing around with a doubleton jack.

Numbly, I awaited inspiration. Again. I was like a zombied-out addict on a street corner, waiting for my connection to show up. What was that fourth hor—

TAKE A ROAD LESS TRAVELED TODAY. THE MAIN CHANCE IS NOT YOUR BEST CHANCE.

Right. That was it.

I am so screwed. I would have killed everybody at the table for a glass of scotch. My little hairs were no longer fooled. My progressively flimsier rationalization had been stretched past the breaking point. The universe *had* done a back flip and things were never going to get better. For a moment I was tempted to do the opposite of the imperative, maybe undo its consequences, but I despaired of that working. What was it Gray used to say? You can't fight City Hall? Well, that must apply to the universe a kajillion times over.

No, now, more than anytime in my life, I was going to need to win to keep me in the liquor and drugs essential to coping. 'Women can help a man forget, too,' a husky femme-fatale voice resurrected from a smoke-filled bar somewhere far, far below the rainbow insinuated mockingly. *Very noir*, I acknowledged. I girded my loins — since my thoughts were momentarily centered there — and dragged myself back to the cards in front of me:

```
      ♠ A 2
      ♥ 5
      ♦ K 10 9 8 6 3
      ♣ —
         ┌─────┐
         │  N  │
         │W   E│
         │  S  │
         └─────┘
      ♠ Q J 9 4
      ♥ J 6
      ♦ 5
      ♣ 9 8
```

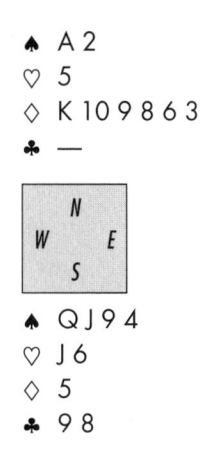

I saw it then, and the drop in blood pressure made me see stars. Fateful stars, aligned by dark forces. *Whoah. That's their plan? Hoo boy. Very... deep*, I conceded ambivalently.

If I was destined to scrape up nine tricks without diamonds, there was only one source left. I cashed the ace of spades. Nothing noteworthy occurred. I would have been astonished if it had. I didn't think Fate would enjoy being mistaken for its dumber cousin, Luck. I called for the two. Crossing the Rubicon. Or rather, flinging myself headlong into the Niagara. With no sign of interest, Lorre played low, as foreordained — my heart didn't even flutter — and I stuck in the nine, assuming — *knowing* — it would lose to Sydney's ten.

It did, and I was at the place where my destiny would fork for good. Or get forked. Except I already knew which. It took a minute, but the king of spades hit the table. Another spade followed.

Wouldn't want to make my jack of clubs a trick, would we, my fellow puppet, I thought sardonically. My apparent nonchalance with the ace of clubs had turned out to be a stroke of genius. Sydney thought I had actually had a reason not to hold up. I obviously didn't have the jack *and* ten or I wouldn't have embarked on my fearlessly nutzoid line of play, which in turn had discombobulated him into fixating on my supposed jack of clubs to the exclusion of anything else. He'd been caught napping like I had last rubber, not counting tricks. An extra club would only be my eighth, and I still had his spade king to knock out. So he too was about to enjoy a head-smacking moment, or whatever form his self-flagellation took. I felt a twinge of guilt knowing he

Weird Scenes Inside the Ol' Mind

wouldn't have the consolation that Fate, taking the form of a momentary blind spot, was what had done him in.

Partner slid out another offering from the diamond mine. Lorre disgorged the jack of clubs.

Silence reigned when it hit the table.

Sydney regarded it for a moment. Then he swiveled his great head, his bright green hyperthyroid orbs locking onto me. One brawny arm slammed down on the table, pumping cards into Mexican jumping beans. My bladder took unilateral action. Then he broke into an astonishingly high-pitched whinny that went on and on accompanied by deep wracking shudders.

He was *laughing*! Killing himself, in fact. He wound down after god-knows-how-long, snorted wetly, dropped his cards face-up. Lorre's six goggling eyestalks split up, dividing their attention between the cards and Sydney. Then he too threw his cards in. This was why:

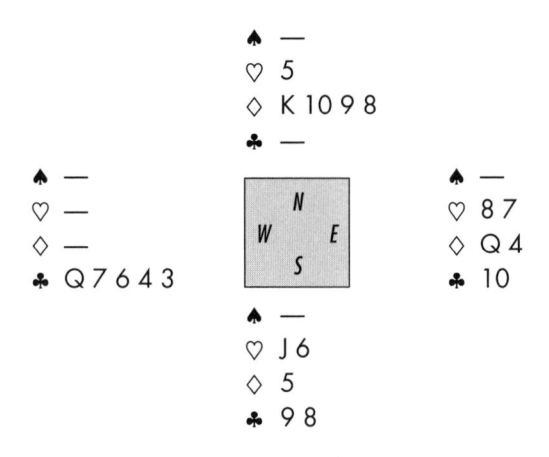

```
              ♠ —
              ♥ 5
              ♦ K 10 9 8
              ♣ —
♠ —                         ♠ —
♥ —        N                ♥ 8 7
♦ —      W   E              ♦ Q 4
♣ Q 7 6 4 3  S              ♣ 10
              ♠ —
              ♥ J 6
              ♦ 5
              ♣ 9 8
```

My next card was going to be a club, and they were finished. If Sydney won, he would have to give me a club trick — and an overtrick, since Lorre would get squeezed on the return. If Lorre won, he'd get to lead into my diamond tenace eventually. Note how absolutely essential it was for Sydney to have the ten of spades. If my nine (or, with his spots, my queen) had forced his king, my obvious three spade tricks would have left him no choice but to assume clubs were wide open. He'd undoubtedly been glad he had that fourth spade to exit with. In my newly minted universe, losing a finesse was a good thing.

Here, for posterity:

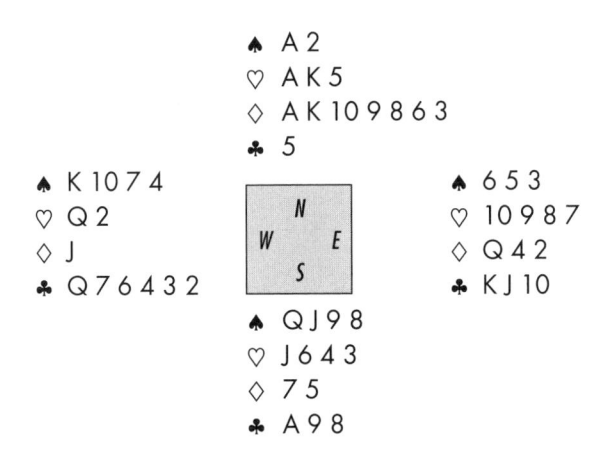

```
                    ♠ A 2
                    ♡ A K 5
                    ♢ A K 10 9 8 6 3
                    ♣ 5
     ♠ K 10 7 4      ┌─────┐      ♠ 6 5 3
     ♡ Q 2           │  N  │      ♡ 10 9 8 7
     ♢ J           W │     │ E    ♢ Q 4 2
     ♣ Q 7 6 4 3 2   │  S  │      ♣ K J 10
                    └─────┘
                    ♠ Q J 9 8
                    ♡ J 6 4 3
                    ♢ 7 5
                    ♣ A 9 8
```

My 'stroke of genius' in immediately winning the club lead was plainly more of a stroke, but I wouldn't have gotten the chance to even the score with Sydney otherwise, would I? Fate was the hunter, but I could tell myself I was one hell of a bird dog. I tried to. Didn't work.

'Oh, excellently played!' he wheezed, meeting my dumbstruck gape. Oily fluid pooled on the ledge of pelt beneath his lidless eyes and overflowed into glistening runnels down either side of his muzzle. Whether it was triggered by laughter or the sting of the ammonia cloud emanating from me, I didn't know. 'What a monumental bluff! Brilliant! And,' he added, 'a tart revenge.' A nictitating membrane in one eye snapped up and down. A wink? It sure looked like a wink.

His fulsome praise didn't go to my head. Machiavelli, aside from having feet of clay, was also sitting in his own urine. My wick-away undershorts — wonderful for those long games when you don't want to interrupt a hot streak — took care of it, but the telltale odor remained.

The lights dimmed briefly to alert us to imminent docking. The two Rigellans that were the other passengers in the lounge heaved to their feet like circus hippopotamuses and lumbered toward the exit, bright orange rolling baggage in tow. Much as I desperately wanted to flee to my cabin — for fresh underwear, if nothing else — I couldn't seem to get my major motor nerves engaged. They were in the grip of *rigor horoscopis*. I was forced to watch, almost dreamily, as the Caroller distentangled himself from his vertical hammock by patting several

Weird Scenes Inside the Ol' Mind

key strands with a clear sap expressed from his abdomen. The strands dissolved, and thus liberated he turned and neatly attended to the rest, straining them through all six sets of fingers and palming the resulting small gobs of grayish residue against his zig-zag mouth to be hurriedly ingested. It reminded me of a praying mantis grooming itself. Done, he tottered off toward the lounge's archway on his bifurcated carapace like he was walking on a set of really starched orange dress tails, without so much as a by-your-leave. He was absorbed into a menagerie of other passengers parading by in the corridor beyond.

Sydney was mostly just sniffling by this time, but every time he looked at me, a soft nickering escaped him. He finally rose heavily and his black formchair melted back into the deck. Mary, still seated, dropped some cards, which struck me as pretty clumsy for a bird of prey, and reached with a taloned foot to pick them up, turning slightly sideways. That was when I noticed how deeply she was sunk in her chair. Not perched, as I'd assumed. Somehow she was a whole lot heavier than she should have been.

Her extended talons morphed into a webbed foot and quickly back again.

She looked up, caught my eye, her body gone still as a startled squirrel. Then her shoulders twitched, a gesture that, had I been forced to guess, I would have described as sheepish.

'HAPPY BIRTHDAY, OLD SOD!' blazed in my brain.

It echoed. How it echoed.

It still does.

I saw the rest as if it were a horror movie I could do nothing but watch. 'She' stood — and transformed from graceful creature of the winds into a heavily built pale-green humanoid with a pockmarked moon face and an unnervingly motile Fu Manchu moustache. The magenta harness criss-crossing the now broad chest pulled apart and slithered to the deck. The new configuration bowed slightly toward Sydney, turned and plodded dignifiedly toward the lounge's arched entrance, sample case abandoned. Turned left into a now empty corridor and disappeared in the direction of the departure area.

All I could manage was a whisper: 'Shoolah...' I've never wanted to move more in my life, to chase him down, but my madly whirring gears wouldn't mesh.

'You know about the shape-shifter?' the Brog demanded in a suddenly reverberating basso growl that pinwheeled my eyeballs.

I worked my way up to a gargle: 'Shape-shifter...?'

'Why would a Ha'dal break the Accord and reveal his ability to you, a...,' — a hesitation — 'a non-Founder? In all the millions of years that they have been our eyes and ears in the Conglomerate, none has ever done such a thing.' He looked away, contemplating something vast. 'The consequences...', he trailed away.

'He's not... who you think he is.' I bumbled.' He talks... to my mind.'

He regarded me again, pointed ears homing in on me in a mannerism I had come to recognize as quizzical. 'You know he cannot communicate in that fashion with one who is not his own kind,' he stated dogmatically, yet with a slight hesitation. 'His *peowr*'—a mellifluous word with no synonym in Galactic — 'organ has no counterpart elsewhere.'

Hysterical laughter ripped my throat open. 'Don't you know... when... the game's... afoot?' I choked out.

Master Point Press on the Internet

www.masterpointpress.com

Our main site, with information about our books and software, reviews and more.

www.masteringbridge.com

Our site for bridge teachers and students — free downloadable support material for our books, helpful articles, forums and more.

www.bridgeblogging.com

Read and comment on regular articles from MPP authors and other bridge notables.

www.ebooksbridge.com

Purchase downloadable electronic versions of MPP books and software.